Also written by Sally Nicol

FICTION

A Model Wife and other tales: A collection of short stories

CHILDREN'S PICTURE BOOK

The chicken who thinks he's a duck

CONTENTS

Introduction

For many years I have shared accounts with friends and family about the sometimes ridiculous situations I find myself in, or the poignant stories I witness in my job as an Occupational Therapist. They have often said, "you should write these down, Sally, it could be a book!"

In this collection I have taken inspiration from the host of people who have given me the privilege of glimpsing something of their own stories. No character is an actual person, but an amalgamation of a lot of individuals, and I have created narratives around incidents that have been described to me or I have experienced myself.

God knows I'm good

The clip holding the hair off her face, positioned just above her temple, gave a guileless impression. She was caught forever in the naivety of middle childhood, generating an instinctive benevolence from those who met her. Whether cultivated for exactly that purpose, it was, nevertheless, effective. Police Community Support Officer Charlie Thomas watched as she crossed the road carefully, her Bag for Life over her arm overflowing with items. Charlie had been walking the streets of Casherbrooke for a few years now and felt he had the trust of the locals. It hadn't taken long, to be honest. Being from a small village himself, he understood the mentality of a close-knit community, where people had known each other all their lives and were a little suspicious of 'in-comers'.

He remembered when Caroline Knight first moved here, about two years ago. Unlike many new people to the village, Caroline drew sympathy rather than suspicion. She did attract attention in her white ankle socks and t-bar shoes, worn with flowing skirts that almost reached her ankles. Though seen as a bit odd, she quickly began to develop friendships when she joined the volunteer group, 'Casherbrooke Companions', becoming one of their busiest helpers.

Charlie crossed the road and followed Caroline into the tea shop. As he entered, he caught snippets of the conversation she was having with the waitress.

"Yes, she seems to be rallying now,"

"Aw, that's great to hear. I bet she was that grateful to you for sitting with her."

"Oh, it's the least I can do. I would be grateful for the company if I were laid up in bed. I do wonder if she'll ever get back down those stairs again though."

The waitress shook her head sympathetically, then spotted Charlie.

"Hiya, Charlie! Coming in to warm up with a cup of tea?"

"That I am, Cassie! And a toasted teacake if you've got one, please."

Charlie took a seat where he could observe Caroline quietly. He saw her slip her plump arms out of her coat and settle herself. He still couldn't imagine there being any cause for concern about the actions of this kindly woman. As far as he could see, she spent all her time offering comfort to the lonely, isolated people of the village. She was popular. Many people didn't even ask for her help through the volunteer agency now but approached her directly - distant sons and worried daughters who felt reassured by the thought of their loved one having regular company and conversation. Caroline was a great conversationalist. She had travelled the length and breadth of the country over the years and had many stories to tell.

Charlie watched as Caroline withdrew an object from her bag. It was a blue elephant ornament, glazed ceramic, expensive-looking. Caroline stroked the smooth surface with her finger, smiling with pleasure. She brought out a woollen scarf and wrapped it around the object, then returned it carefully to her bag. She raised her head and seeing Charlie, called out.

"Hello, Charlie. How are you?"

"I'm good, thank you, Caroline. Busy day?"

"My days are never busy, Charlie, but often full. Busyness would suggest stress and struggling to complete all the tasks. I don't allow myself to get stressed - life is too short!"

"Would you mind if I join you, Caroline?"

"Of course not, it would be lovely to have your company!" Caroline beamed at Charlie and moved her bag to one side.

"Have you been spending then?" asked Charlie, nodding towards the bag.

"No, that's mostly my knitting. I've been to see Joan and I usually take my knitting along. She always talks about the 'Knit and natter' group she used to run years ago, and I like to recreate that experience for her a little."

"What are you knitting?"

"Some hats for the maternity unit."

"You'll get your reward in heaven, Caroline!"

"I get my reward every day, Charlie. I get as much from them as they do from me."

Charlie cocked his head slightly, "How's that, then?"

"I do so love to hear their stories. They haven't always been old, you know. They've lived wonderful, exciting lives. Some have been rather naughty!"

Caroline giggled and brought her hand up to her face to cover her mouth, as a child might do when she thinks she might be caught laughing when she shouldn't be.

"Here you are, Charlie, one tea cake and a pot of tea. And a hot chocolate and slice of toast for you, Caroline. On the house, for both of you - between you, you serve our community well." Cassie smiled gratefully and turned away.

Caroline called "Thank you, Cassie," and lifted her cup to her mouth.

Charlie took a bite of his tea cake and thought back to recent conversations he'd had with people in the village.

The first had been with the daughter of Margaret Buckle, an elderly lady who suffered a bad stroke about 6 months ago. Poor Margaret had lost her speech and the ability to move around her home. A bed had been brought downstairs, and now she relied on carers for most of her day-to-day activities. As was common, the carers were so busy doing the tasks assigned to them that they had no time to simply sit with Margaret, and her family had been concerned that she was becoming very depressed. Caroline had been visiting for the last few months and Margaret looked forward to her visits. But Margaret's daughter had been invited to a wedding recently and asked to borrow her mother's beautiful aquamarine drop earrings. When she'd searched the bedrooms she couldn't find the earrings anywhere. Her mother had indicated that they should be in her jewellery box but they were nowhere to be found. She'd spoken to Charlie of her fears that they had been stolen by one of the carers.

In the same week, Charlie had visited a retired school mistress after he'd noticed a cracked glass pane in her window, offering to get it sorted for her because he was worried about her security. Old Mrs Rafferty had made him a nice cup of tea and shared with him about her many years of teaching. She spoke fondly of her former pupils and colleagues and they'd discussed how people didn't seem to stay in the same jobs for years anymore like they used to.

"Once upon a time you were loyal to your employers and they were loyal to you, too!' she said, 'I was given the most beautiful Wedgewood vase when I retired. You'll see it on the top of the unit there!" She motioned to the wall unit along the wall of the lounge.

Charlie scanned the shelves but could see no Wedgewood vase.

"Can you see it? Take it down and have a look," Mrs Rafferty said, "'t's exquisite. A magnolia design."

"I can't see it, Mrs Rafferty. Perhaps your family has put it somewhere safe."

"Nonsense! It's lived there for thirty years. It's perfectly safe." She stood shakily, supporting herself on her stick, and turned her clouded eyes across the room. She walked slowly towards the unit and squinted at the shelves. Raising her stick, she pointed to the top central shelf.

"It should be there. Where is it, then?"

"What does it look like?"

"It's Wedgewood blue, with white ceramic magnolia. About 12 inches tall."

Mrs Rafferty became upset and Charlie escorted her back to the chair. He'd telephoned her family to ask about the whereabouts of the vase but to no avail. Nobody knew where it could have gone. When questioned about who may have visited the house, only Caroline's name had been mentioned.

"She visits every couple of weeks for a cup of tea and a chat. But it couldn't possibly be her!" Mrs Rafferty had exclaimed, "Could it?"

Charlie now looked over at Caroline, primly eating her piece of toast and brushing the crumbs from her fingers.

"You've moved around a bit, over the years, haven't you, Caroline?"

"Yes, I have. I have no ties as I was never married, and after a while, I begin to feel a little restless so I up-sticks and move somewhere new! Quite the adventurer!'" Caroline giggled.

"And your volunteering? What started you doing that?"

"Well, it's a good way to get to know people when you first move into an area. And there's always such a need. People are much the same everywhere you go, you know. Families living long distances away, people feeling lonely."

"It's very kind of you."

Caroline smiled. "Well, I must get going, Charlie. I'm off to see John Curtis later, and I need to pick up his new books from the library."

She rose to her feet and put on her coat, knocking over her bag for life as she did so. Charlie picked it up and handed it to her.

"Goodbye, Caroline."

As he finished his pot of tea, Charlie felt his foot connect with something under the table. Reaching down, he found Caroline's woollen scarf. Lifting it carefully, he unwrapped the blue elephant and studied it, lost in his thoughts. Shaking his head, he rose to his feet and left the shop. He would drop it at Caroline's after he had done his talk at the primary school this afternoon. He'd never been to Caroline's rented cottage but he did know where she lived.

A little later Charlie rapped the heavy knocker on the wooden door. Caroline opened the door with a beaming smile.

"Charlie! Hello, again!"

"Hello, Caroline. After you left the Tea Room earlier I noticed that this had fallen out of your bag."

He offered the woollen scarf, and the blue elephant separately, so the ornament didn't drop to the floor and break, and so he could observe her reaction to the object.

"Oh Charlie, thank you so much! That's really kind of you. I hadn't missed it but I would have been so sorry to have lost this. Can I invite you in for a cup of tea?"

"No, thank you. I'll be off. Take care!"

"You too!"

Charlie reached the end of the street and then hesitated. He couldn't shake the discomfort he'd been feeling about Caroline, and yet he couldn't bring himself to think ill of this selfless woman who gave all of her time to those in need. But why did she have an expensive-looking blue ornament wrapped in a scarf? If she'd bought it from a shop, surely it would have been boxed or bagged carefully? And if she hadn't just bought it, why would she be carrying it around with her? The delight on her face when stroking it in the tea room suggested that it was new to her. Charlie retraced his steps to Caroline's house and knocked on the door. When she didn't answer, he tried the door handle. The door was unlocked. Rapping again with his knuckles, Charlie stepped into the cottage.

"Caroline?"

He could hear the strains of music coming from upstairs, an old-fashioned crooner singing about love letters in the sand. "Caroline?" he shouted, "It's Charlie. Your door was open."

Following the music, he climbed the stairs, then hesitated at the closed door. Knocking, he turned the handle, "Caroline, it's Charlie…"

Charlie stood in the doorway and took in the scene. Caroline was seated on the floor humming to herself, polishing the blue elephant with a cloth. Pastel blue curtains were closed over the window, and the room seemed to be swathed with hues of blue - bedspread, cushions; scarves hung on the walls. Along the wall were glass cabinets with mirrors at the back, so that every object on display was multiplied. And every object was blue.

Charlie could see a Wedgewood vase placed centrally on one shelf; he saw two or three perfume bottles, exquisitely shaped, on display; a powder blue silk scarf was arranged decoratively beside a cornflower blue handbag; some unlikely-looking blue cowboy boots with rhinestones embedded took up one shelf, and another shelf seemed to be dedicated to jewellery -

Charlie could see some earrings with pale blue, aquamarine stones; a beautiful damselfly brooch and a Kingfisher brooch. A turquoise pendant was displayed on a silver chain.

Caroline raised her head as she became aware of Charlie.

" Charlie! I didn't hear you come in!"

She was startled but showed no signs of guilt or shame.

"Caroline - I knocked but you didn't answer. What is all this?"

"Oh, just my souvenirs."

"Your souvenirs? Caroline, where did you get these things from?"

"All sorts of places!" She stood and took out the silk scarf. "This was given to me by an old lady I used to visit in Leeds. It's an original, made in the 1920s. Isn't it beautiful?"

"Yes, it is. It looks expensive. She gave it to you?"

"Yes, so kind of her." Caroline brushed her cheek with the fabric.

"And these?" Charlie indicated the cowboy boots.

"Haha, yes, the Nashville boots! A life I could have had in another world!"

"Were they a gift, too? Seems an unusual gift."

"Hmmm, I enjoyed the stories that went with them so much."

"Caroline, the Wedgewood vase. It belongs to Mrs Rafferty, doesn't it? She didn't give that to you, did she?"

"Not exactly, no." Caroline smiled shyly at Charlie. "Not yet, anyway. But I expect she would have done, I just didn't want to wait. And she couldn't even enjoy it anymore, with her failing eyesight, so I'm looking after it for her a little early!"

Charlie looked at Caroline in disbelief.

"Caroline, you have stolen some of these objects. From vulnerable people."

"Oh Charlie, don't make it sound so sleazy! I look after them. I honour them, and I know all the stories behind them. These things would just find their way into rubbish bins and charity shops when their owners die, and they deserve better."

"It's theft, Caroline. You can't do this."

"God knows I'm good, Charlie. He won't mind!"

Caroline picked up the elephant and placed it carefully on a shelf.

"Why is everything blue?"

"Blue stands for depth and stability, and it's a calming colour. I love to sit here, surrounded by beautiful things, remembering the stories, holding these objects. It's my reward, you see, for giving my time to lonely people."

"How long have you been … collecting?"

"Oh, most of my life, I suppose."

"Caroline, this is wrong. You do understand, don't you? These things are not yours to keep."

"How can it be wrong to treasure things? To look after them? To enjoy them? I'm not hurting anybody. I only ever take things that people can't use anymore."

Charlie stepped towards Caroline and took hold of her hands with a heavy heart.

"I'll have to radio this in. You do understand what's going to happen, don't you, Caroline?"

Caroline smiled at him. "Of course, you must do as you think best, Charlie. Shall I put the kettle on for a cup of tea?"

As Caroline swept from the room and made her way to the kitchen Charlie surveyed the multitude of objects in the room, from Mediterranean blue, to midnight blue, to sapphires so dark that they appeared black. Would people understand the actions of this child-like woman who felt no self-consciousness in taking things from those in her care? He feared the community was about to be rocked to the core and their loyalties tested to the limit. He withdrew his radio from his pocket and paused, taking some time to consider.....

Condemned

The man held his phone to his ear, head high like a strutting peacock, and proceeded to have a lengthy conversation conducted at such a high volume that the rest of them were forced to listen whether they wanted to or not. Not interested in his misogynistic opinion of his colleagues or his Alpha-male chest-beating, Angela tried to block her ears. What was he doing on the 483 anyway? Probably serving a driving ban and having to slum it on the local transport with people he looked down on. Driving ban – if only that had been an option for John. Prison life will destroy him. How will he ever live a normal life again? She had no idea what she would find when she entered the prison. Will he have forgiven her? Her boy, her sweet baby boy.

Conscious that her emotions were getting the better of her, Angela tried to distract herself, watching the small child climb aboard the bus with her dad. The little girl led the way and chose one of the raised seats, exclaiming with delight "I can see everything, Daddy!" Her father smiled indulgently, infected by her pleasure. As the bus began to move again, the little child giggled "This is so much fun!" Angela watched and wondered whether life would have been different if her children's fathers had been present as they grew up. John had been so confused when his father died when he was just five years old. Having a four-year-old daughter and baby son in addition to John, Angela had little time or energy to answer his searching questions as he grew. Her second marriage had lasted only a few years, producing two more children but little else to provide any stability.

"Don't bump into the cars!" sang out the little girl. "Stooooppp". She giggled at her dad as the bus drew to a halt with a shudder which caused the standing passengers about to disembark to lose their footing.

A car wreck – that's what her life felt like right now.

**

She'd heard the front door slam, followed by heavy footsteps rushing up the stairs. This was not unusual in her house. Two teenagers and a pre-teen meant a lot of hormones were flying around, and her six and eight-year-olds were constantly squabbling. She knew that John had been to show off his new car to his girlfriend, delighted at his achievement of passing his driving test on his first attempt, and at Angela's decision to buy a second-hand car with the money she'd put aside for him after his father died. It was a decision she had regretted every day since. If she had not indulged him he would be at home now with his family. He would have a future to look forward to rather than years behind prison bars. She carried the blame for every decision she'd made from that week on – she was culpable, she had made choices that had determined her son's fate, and there was nothing she could do to make it right again.

**

The bus was getting full now and she had to shuffle along the seat to make room for a large man with a jowly face, shiny with droplets of sweat covering the skin. Bags under his eyes suggested sleepless nights and his mouth was without expression. She wondered what kept him awake at night. Was it guilt, responsibility for another person, or a dependent? Money problems, or stresses at work? His bulk was barely contained within the seat and Angela felt an uncomfortable warmth against her leg where his jogging bottom-clad thigh pressed.

She shifted her position, moving closer to the window, feeling a sudden desire to get away, to turn around. She began to feel panic rising. She needed to get off the bus. She couldn't do it. She couldn't face her son. She'd betrayed him. He would hate her for the rest of his life. Her other children would also hate her. Her sixteen-year-old daughter already did and had made her views very clear. "Why couldn't you just lie, Mum? He's your son, your own flesh and blood. Other mothers would have lied, but not you. Oh no, you have to be all goody-goody and moralistic. Well, how moral is it to betray your own son?"

Sarah's anger was shocking and Angela had no answers because she believed herself to be guilty as charged. She had betrayed John, but what choice did she have? She had four other children that needed her. She couldn't abandon them, there was nobody else to look after them. She would have given her life for John, but not at the expense of the other children. She had sacrificed her firstborn son and refused to lie for him or provide him with the alibi he needed to remove him from the crime scene.

Angela felt sick. She began to gather herself and made to rise from her seat when the man beside her stood and picked his way to the front of the bus as the next stop approached. She stood, frozen to the spot for a moment, and the bus began to pull away from the curb. She opened the window, reclaimed her seat, and stared out, trying to regain her composure.

**

It was probably a couple of hours after he bounded up the stairs that Angela had gone up to see John and ask what his girlfriend had thought of the car. John was sitting on his bed, no music on, not playing on his phone or computer. Just staring ahead, distant and lost. Angela's heart had ached and she closed the door quietly behind her, thinking that she would be dealing with the broken heart of a rejected boyfriend. She sat beside him on the bed.

"Want to talk about it?"

Silence.

"Well, I'm here if you want me. It's not the end of the world though, Son. You'll get through it. It hurts, I know, but it will pass."

"You don't know anything," John whispered.

Angela noticed that John's eyes were filled with tears. She raised her hand to move his long fringe to one side, but he shook her off, standing quickly.

"Stop treating me like a kid, Mum. I'm not a kid anymore."

"I know, I know. But you'll always be my boy, no matter what." She smiled.

"No matter what?" He repeated, his back turned on me. "How can you say that, Mum? It's a stupid thing to say. You don't know what I'll do. Maybe something awful."

"I very much doubt that. You're a good lad, and I'm proud of you...."

"Stop it! Stop it! Will you just stop!" John yelled.

Angela, startled by the rush of anger and confusion in her son's voice, stood and came alongside him in front of the window, watching the traffic pass.

"I killed someone," John said.

**

Now on foot, Angela was nearing the prison gates. A group of people had already gathered, waiting to be allowed entry. As she approached Angela studied them. They were varied, and not all what she'd expected. She'd anticipated that she would feel out of place, that most people would be from a rough background, uneducated, squalid even. She recognised with shame that she had been as guilty of pride and condescension as the strutting peacock on the bus. Most of the people here were just like herself – finding themselves, dazed and confused, in a story they had never anticipated, with somebody they loved behind prison bars. She looked at an elderly couple, probably in their seventies. Who would they be visiting – a son, a grandson? Their hopes and dreams of a fruitful and happy life in tatters. The man stood proudly, daring others to judge at their peril, and his wife fussed with her carrier bag, presumably some treats for the prisoner, some home comforts perhaps? Angela took her place behind them in the queue.

"Are you alright, dear?"

Angela realised that the lady was speaking to her.

"Oh, yes, thank you."

"First time?"

"Yes. Can you tell?"

"I can feel it from you, dear. I know how it feels. Your son?"

"Yes. He's only just turned eighteen."

The lady reached out and took Angela's hand. The tears welled up in Angela's eyes.

"It's so hard. His little brother and sister keep asking where he is all the time and I don't know what to tell them."

"How long will he be here, dear?

"12-14 years". Angela sobbed. It was the first time she had spoken this out loud. So many years. More than half his lifetime. She shuddered to think of the kind of influences he'd be getting here. What kind of man would emerge from this hell hole in 12-14 years' time?

"I have another son who thinks having a brother in prison gives him some kudos. He's bragging about it at school."

The lady squeezed her hand. "You'll get through it, dear, and so will they."

"He hates me."

"That too will pass."

**

"Killed someone?"

"Tonight, in the car." John began to pace the room. "My phone, it was ringing. It'd slipped off the seat into the footwell. I tried to reach for it. It was only for one second. I didn't let go of the wheel. I wasn't going fast. It just happened so quickly. Suddenly, I looked up and she was there, and then I couldn't see her anymore."

"Slow down," Angela said, "so you knocked someone down. Were they hurt? Did you call an ambulance? The police?"

"I was reaching for my phone, Mum. How could I tell that to the police?"

"Wh-who did you knock down? Was it a child?"

"No, an old woman. And will you stop saying 'knocked down' – I didn't knock someone down, Mum, I ran over them."

"Did you get out of the car? Check if she was hurt. this old lady?" Angela had to sit down. Her legs were shaking and she felt nauseous.

"I stopped and looked at her. At first, she had her eyes open and looked at me – it was awful. Then her eyes closed. I looked around, there was no one there, I didn't think anyone had seen, and I was scared, Mum, I didn't know what to do."

"So, you just got back in the car and drove home? Leaving her there on her own?"

John nodded his head.

"Oh John...."

They went downstairs to look at the car. There was blood

and a dent on the bonnet. Together they washed off the blood in silence. Angela didn't get a moment's sleep that night. It was as they were eating breakfast the next morning that the doorbell went and Angela led two police officers into the house. The children quietened when they saw the uniforms and watched in awe as their brother was arrested and charged with the murder of a person that he'd run over and then left the scene of the crime. It had all been captured on CCTV and the evidence was strong.

Sarah had sprung to her brother's defence saying, "No, he was here, wasn't he, Mum? He didn't go anywhere, did he Mum? Mum, tell them! It wasn't him! It couldn't have been him."

Angela had stood, speechless as they led her boy away.

**

In the months since she hadn't seen him other than in court. He'd refused her attempts to visit him and had avoided any eye contact throughout the trial. The longer it continued, the more Angela had felt condemned, not only by him but also by Sarah, who couldn't understand how she had just stood by and let John be taken without a word of support. She'd written him letters but received no reply. It had now been eleven months and her latest application to visit had not been refused.

She walked into the stark room which was equipped with red plastic chairs and small tables. As she entered she passed the elderly couple who were seated opposite a middle-aged man, receding on top, with his remaining hair worn longer as if to prove his ability to grow his mane. The long hair was teamed with unshaved side-burns, which resembled two loofahs affixed to each side of his head. Despite his size and obvious ability to look after himself, he was looking at the lady with tenderness, while her husband looked on, still dignified in his posture.

Angela took her seat at the table allocated to her and watched the door for her son to appear. Weak with trepidation sweat beginning to form on her skin, time stood still, and then she saw John emerge, a prison officer on each side, his wrists in handcuffs. As he approached Angela noted that he sported a black eye and had some stitches across his right eyebrow. Their eyes locked as he approached the table and John said, quietly,

"Hi, Mum".

Uncertain what to say to one another their eyes roamed the room and fell on the elderly couple and their son. The lady was gesturing to John and saying something which they could not hear; the two prisoners stared at one another while their loved ones looked on in hope and in love.

Finding Grace

There's something hauntingly beautiful about a British seaside town in winter. The empty loungers facing out onto a dark, brooding sea under a cloudy grey sky; the marshmallow pink shop fronts straining to cling on to summertime happiness; the floodlit shops selling rock in the darkening skies, open to the elements, with seated shop assistants lonely in their colourful den; the lights of the Amusement Arcades continue to blink, casting shadows infused with red, then green, then yellow, while the first two lines of 'Cotton-eyed Joe' play on repeat competing against the bells and whistles of the other machines for the attention of the occasional visitor.

Ingrid Dixon adjusted her woolly hat over her ears and then breathed warm air into her gloved hands. She felt the cold more nowadays and had stopped taking her regular walks. To be truthful, she had stopped many things in the last six months as she couldn't seem to rustle up the energy or the motivation. She paused beside the stationary Big Wheel looming out of the darkness with its empty carriages silhouetted against the now moonlit sky. A smile flickered across her lips and she closed her eyes, remembering and hearing the delighted squeals of her friends as Vince bounced in the bucket, causing it to shudder and grind.

"Vince," she whispered, "whatever am I going to do without you?"

"Come on," she heard, "'let's go!"

Turning quickly to the voice, she saw a group of teenagers making their way along the Prom. The speaker was a young man of about sixteen, full of life, evidently the 'leader of the pack,' or would that be the local 'Influencer' in today's terminology? Vince had been their Captain. A mercurial character, he could change from being indolent, like a cat lying in the warm sunshine, to a wild and hungry cheetah running in the savannah. His mood was unpredictable and the rapidity of its change could be startling, but he was irresistible to the other young people in this small seaside town. He was her best friend – always had been - and now Ingrid felt lost. Stuffing her hands into her pockets, she started for home.

'"Tomorrow," she whispered into the cold, still air, "I'll start tomorrow."

The next day she opened her curtains and had to look quickly away as the sun glared on the surface of the sea. Looking to her left, she saw the light bouncing off the cliffs of Flamborough Head, looking glorious under a perfect blue sky.

Resolved that today would be the beginning of her recovery, Ingrid picked her coat from the hook and her keys from the table and headed in the direction of the cliffs. Most of the sea birds had left, disappearing into the far ocean, and wouldn't be seen for many months, but there were still a few gannets diving into the water like arrows shot from the sky and fulmars soared on slim wings, riding the thermals effortlessly. The paths were quiet, with only the keenest of walkers out on this cold morning. Pausing to look down to the beach, Ingrid spotted a family of seals on the rocks below, some bloodied around their face, perhaps from a recent fight or maybe the blood of their prey. Most were oblivious to her but one had turned its puppy-dog face and seemed to be staring right back at her. A sudden memory of Vince playfully teasing her when her courage had failed brought a smile to her face. He knew her so well. He'd seemed to be so tuned in to her emotions that he would appear unexpectedly, like Mary Poppins, at exactly the time she most needed him, even after he'd moved away. How did he do that? The memory of this had only compounded her feeling of failure that she had been so blind to his need, guilty of neglecting her best friend.

Ingrid continued her walk, heading inland now, into the more sheltered area. A grey squirrel stopped its foraging abruptly, standing very still, its white abdomen reflecting in the sunshine, its ears the only part of its body showing signs of life as it waited for the danger to pass. Ingrid paused, allowing the creature to move to safety before proceeding. Her eyes followed it as it sped up the tree trunk and her heart lurched as she spotted the reddish-brown, open blades of an old pair of kitchen scissors hanging like a Christmas decoration high up in the branches. Adjusting her position for a better view she gasped, recognising the poppy red handles as they turned in the gentle breeze.

As Ingrid stared, a memory played in her mind of Vince climbing the tree, having snatched the scissors from her hand.

"Vince, give them back!" she'd shouted, uncertain whether to laugh or be angry.

'You don't need them!" he'd shouted back.

"I do! It's up to me what I do with my hair, not you!"

"You don't need to change – I love you exactly as you are! You're better than all of them."

Ingrid had laughed, buoyed by his faith in her, by the dedication and craziness of her best friend.

"But I just want to fit in ..." she'd laughed, her resolve beginning to weaken.

Vince had grinned down at her from the branches, "You don't need to be like them. You're perfect, and if they don't appreciate you just because they think you have an old-fashioned hairstyle, they don't deserve you. And just in case you're tempted again, I'll leave these here!"

Vince hooked one of the handles over the branch. "Whenever you feel inadequate or doubt yourself, you come back here and look at these scissors, and remember that you are the best of them all!"

Ingrid had shielded her eyes and was momentarily blinded, unable to see Vince's face. His unpredictable temperament had changed again, suddenly serious. Before Ingrid could respond, he bounced down from the tree again, flicked her long plait, and scooped up some fallen leaves, throwing them towards her.

Ingrid now gazed at the scissors, amazed that they were still there. She hadn't been here for a long time. She supposed that when the tree was in full leaf, they would be hidden, and even in winter, unless your gaze was directed upwards, you wouldn't notice them.

"I'll bet there's a good story about them!"

Ingrid jumped at the voice and turned to find the source.

Beside her stood a woman of around forty, a riot of colour from her berry-red dyed hair to her navy-blue boots, a voluminous, tangerine, woollen coat covering her neck to her shins. Her lips were painted scarlet and she exuded an inner joy only found in someone completely at peace with themselves. She looked at Ingrid steadily, a reassuring smile on her red lips.

"Yes," Ingrid replied, falteringly.

"Not what you'd expect to find dangling from a tree out here!"

"No," Ingrid returned her gaze to the scissors. "My friend put them there, about twenty-five years ago."

"Interesting! What's the story?"

"He didn't want me to cut my hair."

The woman laughed quietly. "He really didn't, did he? A good friend?"

"The very best." Ingrid, embarrassed, brushed a tear from her cheek. "He died recently. I'm sorry…"

"I'm sorry to hear that. Good friends are hard to come by and precious to have. What was he like?"

"Oh, funny, crazy! Charismatic. Loyal. He was always there for me, all my life, from being at school."

"What happened to him?"

"That's the thing – I don't actually know. He moved away from here when we were in our early twenties, moved to 'the big city," Ingrid made air quotes with her fingers. "We kept in touch and he seemed to have a sixth sense about when I was struggling. When I needed a friend, he was always there. He left just after my wedding but was there for me when my marriage break-up and when the kids left home… We'd talk on the phone regularly, but then …"

Ingrid brought a tissue out of her pocket and blew her nose. The woman didn't interrupt but listened and nodded as Ingrid continued.

"Five weeks ago, he killed himself. Committed suicide."

"Did he have a family?"

"No, he never married. He didn't seem lonely, always the extrovert, you know. People always liked him. But now I'm understanding that all the conversations we had were always about me, my life... I don't know about his life, not really."

"Perhaps that was what he wanted."

"I can't help feeling I let him down. What kind of a friend was I, always wrapped up in myself? He must have been sad, obviously."

"He didn't leave a note? An explanation?"

Ingrid shook her head.

"I suppose, in a way, he left one a long time ago," The woman offered, gazing up at the scissors in the tree. "He left something up there that spoke of his love for you. Twenty-five years ago, you say? And the scissors are still there – look, what do you see?"

Ingrid raised her eyes – the crossed scissors had swung around on the branch and were silhouetted against the blue sky.

"A kiss!" Ingrid smiled.

"A kiss," the woman affirmed, "He wouldn't want you to blame yourself. He sounds like a wonderful person."

Ingrid kissed her fingers and raised them to the sky. "Thank you, Vince. I love you too."

The woman reached out a hand to Ingrid's shoulder.

"I'm Grace," she said, "and I'm here if you need a friend."

"I rather think I might," Ingrid answered as they made their way along the path together. The twigs snapped beneath their feet and neither heard the gentle thud of the scissors as they dropped to the ground when the small branch fell from the tree.

Lessons in love

Rather than heading straight to the station, Giles decided to take a walk through the nearby park. It was 5.30 pm and evenings were still long. A gentle breeze was swaying the leaves of the trees and the park was quiet, most people heading home to begin preparations for their evening meal. He paused when he came to a small clearing where there were a couple of benches. One of the benches was occupied by a woman who wore several layers of clothes, one on top of the other, in the manner of someone without a home to store them. Her hair was long and in need of some attention and her skin leathery as if she spent all of her time outdoors. She was probably about 50 years old but looked older. Beside her was the tell-tale black bin liner that held all the rest of her belongings. Giles avoided eye contact and began to head for the other bench but stopped when he realised that she was saying something to him.

Her voice was like a whisper through a keyhole – it bade you come closer to discover what she was saying. But though the whisper was quiet as if she had not used her voice for a while, there was no hesitancy or lack of confidence – it was a voice designed to demand your attention, as when a teacher lowers her voice in a classroom full of noisy children. She was pointing to something on the ground and Giles saw it was a robin, its red breast looking glorious in the evening sunlight.

"…………symbol of renewal, new beginnings." Giles just caught the end of the sentence and went a little closer.

"We can learn a lot from watching birds. It can help us to gain perspective and teach us lessons about life." she continued.

"Hmm, I have something of a new beginning myself. I've

just become a dad and it's scaring me to death. I know nothing of being a dad."

Standing beside her, Giles watched the robin. It stood motionless for a time and then, suddenly and furtively, ran quickly across the ground, before freezing again. He'd never paid much attention to birds before, much less studied their appearance, and he was mesmerised by the density of the colouring of its breast, the sharpness of its tiny beak. The robin didn't seem too worried about their presence, which surprised him. He commented on this out loud and the woman nodded.

"Some people say they are a sign of a lost relative visiting them, others that a robin is all about perseverance and trying to 'keep on keeping on.' They defend their territory the whole year round and that requires a lot of focus."

Giles had sat down beside the woman so he could better hear what she was telling him, and together they watched the robin.

"What if I mess it up?" Giles mused, to himself rather than his companion on the bench.

Giles lost track of time but as he headed for the station later he felt calmer and during his journey, he wondered if any robins had established territory within his garden at home.

The following evening, preparing to leave the office again, he thought of the strange woman in the park and wondered whether she had made that bench *her* territory for the time being. He strolled to the clearing and yes, there she was. He nodded to her and slowed his pace, looking around him at the treetops, hands in his pockets and feeling a little awkward. He noticed a slightly larger bird on one of the lower branches, its creamy yellow front dotted by black spots, its wings brown. As he watched, it began to sing loudly, joyfully even. Giles listened for a while, transfixed, and then heard the voice of the woman saying,

"If you look closely, those spots are more like little arrows pointing up to the head, as if to say 'listen to me, listen to what I am saying to you.' There is no bird that celebrates life more than a Song Thrush."

Giles listened to the beautiful melodic chorus in the evening sunshine.

"Having a family is all I ever wanted in life. A family of my own. I was so chuffed when Julie told me she was pregnant. Overjoyed!"

"Song Thrushes have inspired humans for centuries. Robert Browning, the poet, said,

'That's the wise thrush; he sings each song twice over,

Lest you should think he never could recapture

The first fine careless rapture.'

A song thrush never allows worrying to stifle its joy", she smiled.

The bird continued to sing and everything else faded to the background as Giles listened. Who was this bird singing to? What purpose did it have? What was the compulsion to sing like this? Did it never tire, grow weary?

On the journey home that night Giles turned the words over in his head, "never allows worrying to stifle its joy". He thought about his delight when Julie first told him he was going to become a father. His incredulity when he held Charlie in his arms for the first time, admiring his perfection, the touch of the soft, downy, wrinkled skin, and that newborn smell that babies have for the first few weeks of their life.

Recently, Charlie had been making soft gurgling sighs of contentment that would break the defences of even the most hardened of hearts. When Giles entered his home that evening his heart felt lighter, as if he had infused some of the joy of the song thrush himself. He wrapped his arms around Julie and swept her around in circles, and they laughed together as they hadn't done for several weeks.

Visits to the park after a day at work developed into a habit then. She was always there as if waiting for him, and she taught him lessons about life, love, joy, and celebration, always using the birds as examples. She explained the importance of family in long-tailed tits, who always stayed together as a group in their spider's web nests that grow as the family grows, learning from infancy the importance of community. They had watched a crow for a long time swooping down to catch an old, hairless remnant of a tennis ball, taking it high in the air and dropping it, determined the break this 'egg' so that it could enjoy a nutritious meal. Each time the crow flew higher and higher, trying to solve the problem, showing persistence and tenacity that was admirable even in its mistaken application.

A mother blackbird had stood atop the roof of an old hut to the side of the path, beak full of mealworms, her understated brown feathers looking astonishingly beautiful. She was calling to her chicks to come and collect their dinner; it was time for them to become more self-reliant and learn about survival. This was the time – it had to be now - no time for hesitation or uncertainty. The survival of her family depended upon her taking control and being decisive. Giles had travelled home that evening with a sense of purpose, strongly resolved to fulfil his role as father to this innocent and completely reliant human being, who would depend upon him for guidance and leadership. The time to step up was now – he could not afford to stand on the sidelines, hesitant and uncertain.

As each of these lessons was absorbed, his agitation and insomnia began to subside. The burden of responsibility that had been crippling him felt lighter and he found that he looked forward to his encounters with the strange woman, finding her presence unexpectedly calming. They'd been meeting each weekday evening for a few weeks and he'd begun to share with Julie some of the lessons he had learned. He'd found that when he began to feel overwhelmed at the weekends with fears or responsibility, spending time in the garden quietly watching the birds about their business had a calming effect upon him. Sometimes he would sit with his son in his arms and remember the insights he had received. Sitting in the garden one day it dawned on him that he now knew the names of many common birds, but he had never sought the name of his teacher. He resolved to rectify this on their next encounter and to ask how he could help her, perhaps financially. He also wanted to ask her permission to take Julie and the baby to meet her.

"I was a wreck," he said, "when I met you that first day. I was ready to run away from it all. Better that than mess up."

The woman stared ahead, saying nothing.

"You were exactly what I needed." Giles glanced at her bin liner on the floor beside the bench. "Is there anything I can do to help you? Do you need money? I'm sorry I've never thought to ask you before. I've been too caught up in myself."

Silence.

"I want to bring Julie and Charlie to see you. Would you mind?"

No response.

"I don't think you know how much you have helped me." Giles squeezed her hand, "You see, I never had a family of my own. My mother abandoned me as a baby, and I never knew why. My dad died while I was still a child, so it was foster homes after that for me."

He paused, shaking his head.

"I would watch my wife as she slept, or my baby boy in his crib, and my heart would race with fear. What if I messed up? Maybe it would be better to leave before I did any damage." Turning to look at her, he said, "I don't even know your name!"

"You can call me Robyn", she whispered, bringing her gaze to him, eyes full of tears.

Giles rose to his feet, gave a little smile, and began to walk away from the bench.'

"A mother always knows when her chicks need help" she whispered.

Hearing her whisper Giles turned and watched her stoop to her bin liner and draw out a small child's teddy bear, give it a kiss and hold it to her heart. "A mother knows, it's just nature."

Stalemate

Her voice was like that of a child, whining, high and shrill, penetrating through every nerve in his body, determined to get his attention and then cling to it like a tick despite his best efforts to extract himself. This had been his whole life, submitting to her will, to her demands. He studied her now frail body in the bed, tissue hanging from bones, thin, grey hair showing her pale scalp beneath, dirty fingernails on veined hands. She disgusted him. There was a faint smell of disinfectant but it was losing the battle with the smell of stale urine and her old, unwashed body. As he looked at her he felt his bile rise and stood abruptly to open the window.

"Don't open the window, Gregory, I'm cold." She whined.

Gregory paused a moment, considering his reflection on the window pane. Fifty-five years old and he'd done nothing with his life except bow to her every whim and desire. He wore his glasses on his forehead in the manner of many middle-aged men, his large ears suitably equipped to support the heavy black frames. His thick lips were surrounded by stubble and his large nostrils focused one's attention firmly on the centre of his face. His lack of shaving had been the first act of rebellion in his life. No teenage uprising from him, no young adult independence, stepping out into the world. Just submission. Complete and abject submission, for fifty-five years, to the will of this woman now lying in bed. He pushed the window open as far as he was able, given the safety restrictions imposed by the unit.

Pulling her blanket up around her she grumbled "I said I was cold."

Gregory, sat once more on the high-backed chair, covered in washable fabric so that urine and excrement could be efficiently cleaned off should an 'accident' arise. He began to unpack the items requested by his mother from his 'Bag for Life': one box of tissues ("not those big ugly, man-size boxes"), one tube of Steradent tablets for soaking her dentures overnight, and one packet of Jelly Babies that he knew she would spend all day picking out of her teeth with her overgrown, filthy fingernails. Well, at least he could walk away and leave her to it rather than have to sit in the same room, fighting his urge to remove the packet and stop the repugnant ritual, whilst at the same time being strangely drawn to watch the very thing that he found so repulsive.

"Did you do the order, Gregory? I bet you forgot didn't you, with your head in the clouds again? You're useless if I'm not there to remind you all the time." she goaded, looking sideways at him with her beady, black eyes.

"Yes, I did the order, Mother, just like I have done for forty-odd years."

"I don't like your tone, Gregory. Don't take that tone with me, while I'm sitting here in bed after an accident. I could have been killed you know."

When Gregory remained silent she continued, "I blame you for it. You always leave things lying around, and never tidy up after yourself. I even wonder if you did it on purpose."

Gregory fixed his eyes on the framed poster on the bedroom wall – a bland, black and white blown-up photograph showing a family enjoying themselves at the seaside. The parents looked on with adoring smiles as the children played with a ball on a sandy beach. Gregory supposed it was to stimulate memories of happy times for those incarcerated within these walls, while they tried to persuade the staff that they were still capable of looking after themselves at home if they were just given a chance. He tried to recall memories of himself, Mother, and Father on a seaside holiday, enjoying time together. He supposed there may have been one or two, but those memories had been buried by the seemingly endless years of servitude since.

"Are you listening to me, Gregory, or are you having one of your silly daydreams again? That's always been the trouble with you, daydreaming instead of facing up to your responsibilities"

Gregory looked at his mother. She had been in the unit for two weeks now, having been transferred there following the fall. They were talking about sending her home again in a few days and he wasn't sure he could take it. In this time away from her he had been thinking about his life and what could have been. He had eaten out in the pub a couple of times and chatted with some of the men who sometimes came into the shop. They'd invited him to play darts with them, even bought him a pint! He'd returned home after 10.30 pm feeling giddy with happiness and nobody had complained to him or demanded to know where he had been and who he had been with. It was the first time Gregory had been alone. It was also the first time he remembered not feeling lonely. He'd eaten when he felt hungry, shaved if and when he felt like it, and discovered his voice again, chatting to customers with a lightness in his spirit that he'd never felt possible. As he gazed at Mother now, watching her pinched, thin lips expel their poisonous words, he wondered whether he could go back to that life. A life strangled by the will of this woman before him.

Bringing his eyes back to the black and white poster on the wall he remembered Jennifer. He'd met her when he was in his teens. Sixteen years old and he was head over heels in love, delighting in her smile and revelling in every moment spent with her. They had lain in the grass in the local park, planning their lives together. He'd taken her auburn curls in his hand and wound them around his third finger on his left hand, promising that he would love her forever. They'd planned on children and even agreed on their names! Those were the happiest days of his life. Then, one week later, his father's death put paid to that. Mother needed him every minute of every day, jealously keeping him at home on some pretext or other. If Jennifer came into the shop Mother would be rude to her, insulting even, commenting critically and loudly on her choice of dress, the amount of make-up she wore, and even the way that she spoke. Gregory had tried to defend his sweetheart privately but he was no match for his mother, impotent in his submission to her stronger will. Jennifer had given up waiting for him and was soon married and beginning a family of her own.

He and his father had planned for him to go away from home to university, to be independent and free, to make his own way in the world, but Mother had stopped that too. Now it was just the two of them, she said, they needed to stick together. University! Of course, that was out of the question now – she would need his help running the shop. So he'd stayed at home, setting aside his dreams.

Some hope entered his life in his mid-thirties when he became increasingly friendly with a customer who shared his interest in art. She'd invited him to join her at the local art club and he'd furtively gathered together his materials, telling Mother that he was doing some deliveries, and managed to join her at a couple of sessions, but word got back to the shop and before long, Mother took over the orders and arranging deliveries, and he no longer had an excuse to leave the house. She made sure that the deliveries were on any night but the night of the art club.

Gradually, over the years his world became smaller and smaller, and he rarely left the house unless Mother was with him. Mother never really ailed and so didn't need Gregory's physical help, but nevertheless, she depended upon him. They didn't have conversations exactly. In truth, Gregory had lost his voice – he used it rarely and when he did, Mother generally talked over him.

Had she always been like this? Gregory tried to remember what she had been like when his father was alive. His father had been an affable chap, a reserved man who spoke only when he needed to. He supposed that Mother had always been the talkative one, but was her talk always so poisonous? To that, he had no answer.

"Are you listening to me, Gregory? I said I want you to make me more comfortable on this bed. I need to sit up a bit more. Make yourself useful, for once."

Gregory straightened his long limbs and approached the bed. Bony hands landed on his wrists with a vice-like grip, cold as steel to match her heart, he thought.

"Snap out of it" she hissed.

He wrapped his arm around her thin back and pulled her up the bed.

"Now sort the pillows out," she commanded.

Gregory removed both pillows from behind her. She sat forward so he could better position them. He tucked the first pillow behind her shoulders, then lifted the second. Their eyes met, steely black eyes filled with venom locked with his impassive gaze. Stalemate. Gregory adjusted his grip on the pillow as he stooped down, and their eyes remained locked. As he leaned into the pillow Gregory turned his face to the poster. The face of the woman became that of Jennifer and the man, his own, and Gregory thought of what could have been, as he extinguished what should never have been.

No secrets

"We have your telephone number, and we'll ring you when we know more," the voice was gently reassuring, "Keep your phone near you, Mrs Atkinson, so you can hear us when we ring."

"Thank you," Phoebe replied, tearfully.

She dropped her trembling hands to her lap and stared ahead. She could see two more ambulances turning into the hospital grounds, preparing to join the three already queued at the entrance to the Accident and Emergency department.

She felt the bench give slightly as another woman sat.

"Do you mind if I sit here a while?" she asked, "I'm just waiting for my taxi." She used her elbow crutch to point to her ankle, heavily dressed with clean white bandages.

"Not at all," Phoebe replied, giving a weak smile.

The two women sat silently and watched the ambulances join the queue.

"It's bedlam in there," the woman said, "'he staff are running around from cubicle to cubicle. They clearly need more staff. If you're waiting for someone, I'd find somewhere a bit warmer if I was you."

"I don't want to go," Phoebe answered, "my sister's in there, but they say she's going straight up to a ward. I should be with her. They won't let me in - this stupid bloody Covid! She's on her own and she'll be so frightened."

"What's happened? Has she had an accident?"

"No, they think it's a stroke. She looked so terrible..." Phoebe's voice began to quiver with emotion. "We're twins, identical. Seven minutes between us."

"Are you the eldest?"

"No, Lizzie is."

"Can people tell you apart?"

"Only a very few people have ever managed that! Our parents of course, and my husband. I think even Lizzie's husband had to wait until we gave him clues sometimes. We used to run rings around people." Phoebe smiled at the recollection.

"You played tricks? I've heard about twins doing that," the woman laughed.

"We were very naughty actually! When I think of the things we did!" Phoebe shook her head with a chuckle. "Sometimes we would swap dates!"

"What! Tell me more!"

"It was mostly Lizzie that instigated it! You would expect her to be the sensible one, being the eldest, wouldn't you? But oh no, that was not the way it was with us! She's always been a bit of a live wire, spontaneous, daring. The first time was when we were 17, she'd been on a few dates with a lad from her office, and he'd bought tickets for the theatre for a show she'd never heard of and didn't really fancy. There was a party going on that she thought would be more fun, so she sent me to the theatre with him while she went out dancing!"

"Didn't he know?"

"No, he didn't! We've always had the same hairstyle. Some people don't understand that - why don't you change your hair so we can tell you apart - but the point was, we felt like we were two sides of the same person. We wanted to look like each other, we needed to see what we saw in the mirror or it would have messed with our heads! We do wear different shades of lipstick though - she prefers a peach and I prefer pink. Anyway, the date went great - we sat in the theatre and enjoyed the show, and I only allowed him a quick peck on my cheek at the end and said I had a headache. Once we knew it worked, we did it a few times - mostly to get Lizzie out of something she thought would be too dull!"

The woman was listening, aghast, amused, and intrigued. Phoebe continued.

"There was only one time we did it the other way round, when I was about 19 and had just started going out with Jacob - who is now my husband by the way! I'd had a couple of dates with him, then was asked out by my boss at work. He was quite a looker and I wanted to test the water, so to speak. I didn't want to mess things up with Jacob because I did like him, but thought, why not just have one date with Gerry to be sure? Lizzie stepped in for me. She wasn't too keen at first but when she got home she said she'd had a great time, and if I decided to choose Gerry, she'd be happy to have Jacob!"

"And Jacob didn't cotton on?"

"Well, we've laughed about it a lot over the years. He says he knew something was not right straight away. I'm a little more reticent than Lizzie and she didn't do a good job of hiding her boisterousness! He says he knew all along that it wasn't me but played along, seeing it as a game or some kind of test. At the end of the evening, he just gave her a peck on the cheek and thanked her."

"Well, this looks like my taxi," the woman stood and began to hobble to the car, "I hope Lizzie is ok. I'll send a prayer up for her."

"Thank you. I hope you are soon better too. Take care."

Phoebe checked her phone for messages and then rang Jacob.

"Hi love, I think you might as well come to get me. They won't let me in and it might be ages before we have any news.' She began to cry, 'Oh Jake, poor Lizzie."

"I'll be right there."

Ten minutes later, Jacob pulled up beside the curb, got out of the car, and swept Phoebe into his arms, squeezing her and stroking her hair.

"Come on, love. Let's get you home and get a nice cup of tea. There's nothing you can do here. She's in the best place."

The next few weeks went by in a blur. It was impossible to get a direct answer to many of her questions and Phoebe hated that all communication had to be by phone. The staff on the ward explained that Lizzie had indeed suffered a stroke and that it had affected her speech as well as her physical capabilities. Eventually, a Multi-disciplinary meeting was held by Zoom to discuss the plans for Lizzie's discharge. Phoebe was introduced to a group gathered in a hospital room, and she could see Lizzie sitting in what looked like a wheelchair. Lizzie looked thinner and her hair had a neglected appearance - Phoebe felt the tears well in her eyes and struggled to remain calm. The camera was angled in such a way that, although Lizzie could be seen, she was furthest away from the laptop, meaning Phoebe could not get a clear impression of her sister's condition. ' Sitting at the back as if she's the least important person in this conversation,' Phoebe thought to herself, 'She should be front and centre.' She was comforted by the thought that her own face would be larger on the screen in the room with Lizzie and she would be able to see Phoebe clearly.

"Thank you for joining us, Phoebe,' said the man who seemed to be taking the lead. 'First, shall we all introduce ourselves?"

Phoebe was introduced to a Physiotherapist and Occupational Therapist, who explained that Lizzie had worked extremely hard and was now mobile again, though using a four-footed stick and with only a little recovery of her arm. A Speech and Language therapist then began to explain that any meaningful speech had been lost completely, although she could understand when others spoke. The stroke had robbed her of the ability to express herself, leaving her with a jumble of sounds. Phoebe had recorded daily voice notes on WhatsApp for the nurses to play to Lizzie, telling her about her day and the family, sending love from them all, and the therapists said this had been very helpful. When asked what she would like to happen, Lizzie began to speak. Phoebe could not hear her clearly but it sounded like she was saying 'Jacojacobjacojake', repeatedly, shaking her head with frustration and humiliation. The decision was made that Lizzie would be discharged to live with Phoebe and Jacob for the foreseeable future. Widowed for the last 5 years, it was impossible for her to return to her home unsupported. The discharge would be planned for in two days' time.

"Oh Jake, it was so awful," she said when he got home from work. "Lizzie was right there and everyone was just talking about her, planning her life, as if she wasn't even in the room. When she did talk she just babbled and didn't make any sense. I'm going round to her place later to start collecting her stuff to make her room look more personal."

"Do you want me to come?"

"No, it's ok. You watch the match, I'll be fine. Lizzie might feel like she's lost even more of her dignity if she thinks you've been rifling through her things as well!"

She was almost finished when Lizzie's cosmetics bag slipped from her fingers and the contents spilled out on the floor. Following the peach lipstick as it rolled under the bed she felt her hands brush against a box about the size of a book, which she drew out with the lipstick. The box was old - indeed Phoebe recognised it as the box which contained the silver decorative horseshoe given to her on her wedding day by Lizzie and her boyfriend Philip, who later went on to become her husband. Sitting on the bed, Phoebe smiled.

"Fancy you keeping this!"

Taking the lid off the box, she found a collection of items and photographs. Lying on the top was an old black and white photograph of Lizzie with Jacob, taken on Phoebe's wedding day. Lizzie was wearing her bridesmaid's dress and Jacob was smiling down at her. Phoebe smiled as she recalled the day and was filled with gratitude that she had married this kind man who had lavished her with love from the day they met. The photograph was a bit dog-eared as if it had been handled often.

Setting it aside on the bed, Phoebe reached into the box and held a piece of tissue paper wrapped around something very light and fragile. Opening the tissue slowly, Phoebe saw the delicate petals of a peach rose that had been carefully pressed. Alongside the petals was a small card which read 'Lizzie, you are one in a million! Love ya!', written in Jacob's handwriting. Phoebe remembered thirty years earlier when the children were young and she'd suffered from a bout of post-natal depression. Lizzie had come to stay for a while and helped with the children. She recalled Jacob coming home with a huge bunch of peach roses and thanking Lizzie for all her help.

Next Phoebe withdrew an old theatre ticket - the ballet, 'Coppelia'. Their thirtieth birthday presents to each other. They'd looked forward to the evening for months, then Phoebe had been unable to go because one of the children was ill. She had tried to pass the child to her father but she was having none of it. She screamed and clung, and in the end, Phoebe sent Jacob to the ballet instead. It wasn't fair for Lizzie to miss out, and they couldn't waste the tickets.

The final item in the box was a cotton handkerchief. Phoebe instantly remembered it as one belonging to Jacob, the Star Wars insignia in the corner was always a bit of a giveaway. Why would Lizzie have this? Closing her eyes, Phoebe began to recollect an image of Lizzie, desperately upset at their father's funeral, and Jacob giving her a brotherly hug and offering her his handkerchief.

Why did Lizzie have all these things in a box beneath her bed? And why did all the items have a connection to Jacob? Looking around the room, Phoebe could find few mementos of Lizzie's husband, Philip. A small photograph in a gilt frame of them in their twenties. A painting he made in retirement still hung on the wall. Phoebe thought about Lizzie and Philip - their marriage had come very quickly after her own to Jacob. Philip was a kind man, a quiet man who tended to blend into the background. She was sure that Lizzie had loved Philip, but it had never been a passionate love like she shared with Jacob.

She thought back to her conversation on the bench outside A&E a few weeks earlier. Lizzie had switched and taken her place on a date with Jacob right at the beginning. Had she fallen in love with him? Had she loved him from afar for all these years? She began to replace the objects in the box, the secret box which had been hidden underneath the bed. A box which had been opened regularly, if the condition of the photograph was anything to go by.

A secret box! But they were twins, inseparable, without any secrets. They'd always told each other everything, hadn't they? How should she react? She would not be able to get any sensible explanation from her sister - that was impossible now. Phoebe gently placed the box into the 'Bag for Life' and closed the door behind her.

Lizzie arrived with the Occupational Therapist, who went on to check that she could manage safely in her new home. Phoebe had used many of the items from Lizzie's home to personalise the room and make it feel as comfortable as possible. The sisters sat quietly holding hands once left alone, and smiled into each other's eyes.

"It's so good to see you, Lizzie."

"Jacobjakyjacojake," Lizzie shook her head in frustration, and tried again, "Jacojake."

A tear trickled out of the corner of her eye and she shook her head violently.

"It's ok, Lizzie. We'll get there. There's all the time in the world. It must be so annoying for you. We'll maybe create our own language, based on how many Jacob's we use!"

Lizzie laughed.

"I hope you like the way I've done your room. It was so hard to know which of your things to bring. We can always go back and get other stuff if we need it. You know you can stay here as long as you like."

Phoebe stood, knelt down on the floor, and brought a small, book-sized box out from beneath the bed. She turned to look at Lizzie, who looked at the box and her sister, and whose tears began to run more freely.

"I thought this should come with you. I wasn't prying, your lipstick rolled under the bed, I came upon it by accident."

"Jacobjakyjacojake," Lizzie held out her hand, not for the box but to grip her sister.

"It's ok. He doesn't know, he doesn't need to know. It's just us, our secret. I'm going to put the box back here, where it belongs. I love you, Lizzie. I don't mind. I'm sorry you couldn't be happier with Philip."

"Jacojake, Jacojake."

Phoebe knelt on the floor and slid the box back underneath the bed. "Whenever you want to look at them, you must tell me. You will ask, won't you? Perhaps we could get a frame for the photo so you can see it whenever you want."

Phoebe dropped a kiss onto her sister's head. "I'll leave you to settle in for a while. Jake and I will bring you some tea and biscuits. Welcome home, darling."

Phoebe quietly closed the door behind her as she left the room.

The last ritual

1996

Chapter one

The kitchen resounded with noise as Babs whisked up the Dream Topping and the girls howled with laughter at the antics of their father. Babs looked over at Paul who was wearing his Christmas apron with Father Christmas and a snowman posing together amiably, full of festive cheer. Laura, now twelve, had done her utmost to resist joining in the fun and maintain her disdain for such childishness but, as always, Paul had won her over.

"Can I have pancakes, Dad?" Ria asked, jumping up and down on the spot.

"Pancakes are for Lent, not Christmas!" Paul retorted, but then swept up his little girl and spun her round, "but Christmas is for treats, so who cares!"

Babs spooned the topping onto the trifle, smiling to herself. "Best make it quick though. We've got a long journey ahead."

"Is that a complaint?" Paul asked, sharply.

"No, of course not," Babs responded quickly, "I just don't want us to be late. Your Mum will have gone to a lot of trouble for us all."

"I doubt Robert and Holly will be worrying about that," Paul grumbled before switching on the charm as he faced the girls again.

"I expect it will depend on how settled Timmy is. He's only

seven months old after all." Babs recoiled slightly at the look Paul threw her and her hand began to shake as she picked up the chocolate sprinkles.

"I'm going to show everyone my new dance," announced Ria, proudly. "Did you remember to pack my dancing costume, Mum?"

"Yes, darling, it's in the case in the hall."

Laura placed a protective hand on the folder on the table beside her. She hadn't yet fully decided whether she would share her drawings with her wider family. The only person who'd seen all of them was her Dad, her great supporter, the one person who seemed to understand her need for solitude. He would sometimes knock on her bedroom door and just sit on the floor, neither of them talking very much, but bonding in the silent presence of each other. Eventually, he would look up from the floor and ask what she was doing. She would shyly slide her drawing from the desk and he would take it from her, nodding, sometimes with tears in his eyes, such was his pride. Laura's drawings were raw, filled with confusion – Expressionism, her Art teacher had called it, art that expressed the artist's inner feelings. Dad would never ask her to explain them, whereas Mum, on the very odd occasion she was shown a drawing, would try to understand, would want explanations that couldn't be given.

"Did you find the scrapbook?"

"Yes, it's with Ria's costume."

"I'm sure Michaela will trump us again this year with some weird and wonderful way of summing up 1996," moaned Paul.

Babs thought there was a mixture of pride and irritation in

Paul's voice. His relationship with his older sister was complex. He relied upon her respect but resented that she seemed to see him with more clarity than perhaps anyone else in the family. Being six years older than him, she had observed him throughout his whole life and was not easily fooled by his charm or affected ways. Babs had sometimes been tempted to confide in Michaela, the most likely member of the family to understand, but had faltered at the possible consequences.

"Da-dah!" Paul flipped the pancake in the air, the flips becoming ever more impressive in height and with Michael Jackson-style manoeuvres in between.

The girls laughed and Ria bounced up and down in excitement, her Christmas pyjamas a blur of seasonal red and green.

Sam stood at the kitchen door, surveying the antics of his family. He watched his father clowning and his younger sisters enjoying this Christmas breakfast. He saw his mother smile lovingly at the scene and he felt fury in his belly.

Chapter two

Eve straightened the eiderdown on her bed, smoothing out the creases. It was still early but she had a lot to do and of course, things took so much longer now. Pressing her palm to her arthritic hip, she stood erect, took a few seconds to establish her balance, then made her way downstairs. Francis was already up, bringing the extra chairs in from the shed. Eve was glad he had Mark's help this year and was proud of her thoughtful daughter Michaela, who had insisted they drive down on Christmas Eve.

Eve always looked forward to Christmas day. Her three children had scattered across the counties, each with successful careers and busy family lives. She didn't see as much of them as she would like, so spending Christmas Day and Boxing Day as a family each year was a real treat. She was delighted they'd managed to keep the family tradition of sharing memories of the year together and was always astonished at the creativity shown.

Last year, Michaela and Mark produced a cine film capturing special moments of their year – volleyball on the beach in Majorca, the twins' performances in the school orchestra, the girls' return from a school exchange trip to Germany – all long hair and violin cases in the exciting family reunion, captured by Mark on his camcorder. Eve couldn't be more thrilled by these two beautiful teenage girls, and Michaela had found gold in her choice of husband. Mark was a civil servant like his wife and was a solid, dependable man.

When was the last time she had seen Paul and Babs? It must be almost a year! Eve had warmed to Babs the moment Paul had brought her home – a gentle, dark-haired girl with a surprising tattoo on her shoulder which Eve only saw for the first time on her wedding day. She was a quiet, peaceful presence, which Eve thought was a perfect tonic for Paul who, as a police detective with the homicide team, saw the very worst of life. Paul was such a smooth operator he could have people eating out of his hands within minutes. She honestly couldn't see how any criminal could get away, with Paul on his case! He had a way of disarming people, using his handsome smile and wit to gain their trust. Her middle child, she had striven to ensure he'd not felt neglected, or overlooked, because of his older sister and younger brother. Sometimes Francis felt she had over-compensated.

And then there was her baby, Robert, and his wife Holly, who would be bringing little Timmy to meet them for the first time. Holly had, thus far, lived up to her name – a little prickly and difficult to get close to. To be fair, they'd not spent a great deal of time together so Eve was trying not to be too harsh. She understood that the struggle to conceive would have taken its toll and hoped that Timmy's arrival would lead to a softening of those sharp edges. Eve had no idea how Robert managed to run his small medical practice and still be so present for his wife and child but somehow he did. He had boundless energy and seemed to pack into each hour what would take a normal person at least double that! Eve shook her head smiling. The family was everything and she had the best.

Michaela was setting up the screen in the living room and the men were assembling the extra table and chairs for the meal. Eve went into the kitchen to begin the preparations for the best day of the year.

Chapter three

"I hope you're not going to have that face on you all day!" Paul said, locking eyes in the rearview mirror with his disgruntled son.

Sam averted his eyes and looked out of the window, watching the spray rise from the ground as cars sped along the motorway.

"It's Christmas Day!" Babs said, "Where are all these people going?"

Laura sighed at her mother's lack of realisation of the absurdity of what she had just said.

"Er, probably visiting family, like us."

She wriggled, trying to find more space in the cramped back seat. Why did she always have to sit in the middle?

Sam spread his legs out wider, staking his hold over the space, while still staring out of the window. She turned round to check that her drawings were still safely on the boot shelf, and received a sharp dig in the ribs from Sam.

"Ow," she shouted, "Dad, Sam's hurt me."

"What's up with you today, mate?" Paul asked.

"Nothing."

"Well, it's Christmas Day and I don't want you spoiling it for everyone, alright? Make an effort."

There was something in Paul's tone that made Sam meet his eyes in the mirror. For a moment, they held each other's gaze, a silent stand-off between father and son, then Paul winked, slapped his hand on the steering wheel, and began singing 'All I want for Christmas is you-ooo-ooo....'

Babs flinched when Paul's hand struck the steering wheel and this was noticed by Sam. Ria joined in the singing with Paul, and after a few feeble seconds of resistance, Laura added her voice to the others and the mood in the car lightened.

Sam struggled with his contradictory and confusing feelings. He simultaneously hated his father with all his heart and wanted to kill him, whilst also finding it hard to quash the pride he'd always felt in this man who turned up to his football matches and proved so popular with the other kids. Having a father who was a police inspector had given Sam a degree of kudos and Sam enjoyed basking in his reflected glory. Whenever his Dad was home when schoolmates were around, he would switch on the charm and have them all laughing, being one of the lads, and nothing like the boring, authoritarian fathers the others had.

But over the last few months, Sam's eyes had been opened and he was shocked to the core.

He was equally baffled by his feelings for his mother. He knew his mates loved her, confided in her sometimes, made excuses to go downstairs for a drink of water, and wouldn't come back for half an hour or more. He was pretty sure one or two of them fancied her but he didn't like to linger on this!

She was always patient with Sam and he knew she would do anything for him, but now he felt a crushing disappointment in her. He'd thought her a strong woman so why didn't she do something? Why didn't she stop it? Why didn't she notice that he knew?

His teacher at school had sensed that Sam had become more withdrawn, more easily startled by sudden noises, and anxious. She'd asked him to stay behind after class a few weeks ago and tried to coax him into telling her how he was feeling. He liked her and didn't want to be ungrateful, but of course, he couldn't tell her. He gave some excuses and made an extra effort to appear 'normal' in class, afraid that she might contact his parents.

And now he had a plan, but could he go through with it? He rubbed his clammy hands against his jeans and tried to concentrate on the rain outside his window.

Chapter four

They were the last to arrive and as they made their way up the drive laden with presents and offerings for the table, they were greeted by the others with hugs and kisses.

"Oh darling, how good to see you, Son."

"Hi Mum," Paul picked his Mum off her feet and gave her a bear hug.

"Babs, I love your silk scarf – it's such a beautiful colour!" Michaela said, taking the trifle from her sister-in-law.

"Aw, look at you! You're so cute!" Ria reached up to Timmy, nestled in Holly's arms.

"What've you got there, love?" Francis asked Laura, looking at the folder.

"Oh, nothing, Grandpa, Happy Christmas!"

People, presents and food were bundled into the house out of the cold, coats removed and alcoholic refreshments provided. Before long all were seated around the tables, tucking into Christmas dinner.

"I hope you've all come prepared!" said Francis with a wink of his eye. "It's my favourite part of the whole thing, hearing about what you've all been up to over the last twelve months."

"Our lives really aren't that exciting." Laura said.

"Maybe it doesn't feel exciting to you, love, but we are always interested in what is happening in the lives of those we love. It's a Gibson tradition! A ritual we've done since your Dad was a lad!"

"It's a lovely tradition," said Babs, "and we've all been thinking how best to show you."

"Have you done another film, Mark?" Paul joked, "Should we be calling you Steven Spielberg and buying popcorn?"

The family laughed but Mark was never quite sure that the things Paul said were meant with complete benevolence, so he felt a little awkward. He smiled and concentrated on his lunch.

"We're going to give you some excerpts from our concerts over the year, with a little explanation about each event," said one of the twins.

Not wanting to be outdone, Ria bounced on her chair, "And I'm going to show you all my dances!"

"Fantastic!" said Eve. Turning to Laura, she asked "What about you, Laura?"

"Um, I've brought some drawings."

"Ah, the file!" Francis tapped the side of his nose and winked, gaining a slight smile from his granddaughter.

"I think you can already guess what our last year has been made up of!" Robert said, nodding towards his beloved little boy, asleep on Holly's shoulder while she ate her meal with her fork.

"Why don't you put him down while you eat, love?"

"It's fine, Eve," Holly answered.

"Or I could take him from you for a while?"

"It's fine, honestly."

"Come on, little Timmy, come to Grandma."

"He's asleep and I said he's fine." Holly's voice was low but snappish and the room fell into an awkward silence.

"What about you, Sam? You prepared to tell us what's been going on in your life?"

"I haven't decided yet, Grandpa."

Everybody laughed nervously.

The table was eventually cleared and people drifted into the lounge. Seats were arranged to give everyone a view of the 'stage' area at the front and feet were trodden on as they made their way to the seats in the restricted space.

"Hope there's not a fire," muttered Holly.

Mark and Michaela set the proceedings off with their film show, which included footage of the twins' concerts.

"I thought the girls were doing the concert thing! Are we going to have to sit through a double dose?" goaded Paul.

Michaela shot him a dark look and reached out a hand to soothe the embarrassed girls.

"It's just a snippet, Paul."

Ria performed her dances and the girls their music, then Babs passed around the beautiful scrapbook she'd made, which included theatre tickets, cinema stubs, school concert programmes, and occasional local newspaper cuttings. One of the cuttings was a picture of Sam with four other students, who had been hand-picked from school to keep a Teenage Diary, documenting their lives for a year. This created a lot of interest and Sam was bombarded with questions.

"Is it a written diary?"

"What will you do with it?"

"Does anyone get to see it?"

"Um, it's a sort of recording. We've all been given a tape recorder and cassettes. We're supposed to speak into it and talk about how we're feeling, what we think about stuff."

"Will people hear it, though?"

"Wow, you're brave. I wouldn't want anyone to read my diary!" The twins looked at each other in horror.

"Well, it's up to me. The point is to sort of see if it helps. It's not what you say but how it makes you feel."

Sam began warming to the topic, bolstered by the alcohol he'd been covertly adding to his pop during the course of the 'show and tell', easy for him as he was seated at the extremity of the group.

"Inside the mind of a sixteen-year-old boy – that's a murky place to go!" joked Paul. "I'll bet it's all a bit x-rated, eh, Son? I know what was in my head when I was sixteen."

"I think he needs a change," mumbled Holly, standing with the baby.

Babs, seated beside Paul on the opposite side of the room, longed to give her embarrassed son a consoling touch.

"Time for some Christmas cake and a top-up of drinks," Francis announced, giving Eve the thumbs up.

Sam reached below his seat and pulled out his rucksack. Slinging it over his shoulder, he left the room and sat on the bottom stair, heart pounding and thoughts racing. He waited until everybody was seated then slipped in, sliding the tape recorder underneath the armchair after pressing 'Play.'

Chapter five

Sam's recorded voice travelled across the room, stilling the conversation.

"Discovering who you are is a strange thing because you can be lots of different people at the same time and because people will only see what you want them to see. I started this teenage diary because I like my teacher and she thought it would be good for me. I began by speaking into my tape recorder and talking about how it felt when my team won at football; How it felt when things were good at school; how I felt when I asked a girl out and she said yes, or she said no. That was when I thought I had a normal family, but then things changed...."

The family began to look uncomfortable, and Paul began searching the room for Sam with his eyes.

"because then I heard this......"

The recording was silent for a few seconds then there was the sound of a hard slap and a gasp of pain from a woman. Something like a table scraped on the floor then crockery smashed. Paul's voice was distinctly heard...

"Go on then, you pathetic, stupid tart, turn the waterworks on – see if I care!"

"Paul, I'm sorry. I didn't mean to upset you."

"Upset me! Upset me! You humiliated me in front of my colleagues."

"I thought you'd like some home-cooked food..."

"When I am at work I need respect from my team, get it? Not them laughing at my little woman bringing me warm quiche!

Respect. Respect. Respect."

With each utterance of the word, there was a dull thud, as if a head was being knocked against something hard, followed by the sound of feet scrabbling to get some purchase on the floor. Babs cried out as she was winded by what appeared to be a blow to the stomach.

"Paul, please ....."'

Another crash as if a chair or a stool was thrown.

Paul was trapped in the corner of the room listening to the tape, on his feet but with multiple bodies between himself and Sam.

"Turn it off!" Paul yelled.

Sam stood his ground at the door.

Babs was trembling in her chair.

Francis was embracing Eve, who was crying. The twins exchanged glances that were a mixture of horror and excitement.

Michaela, who was closest to Sam, said, "Where is it? Where's the tape recorder? That's enough, Sam, turn it off."

Sam didn't respond.

Mark and Robert began searching the room and still the recording played, now Sam's voice.

"I've always thought my Dad was the best. He's funny and popular, everybody loves him. But he's a monster and this isn't the only time he's hit Mum. It's getting worse but she's still here. Why are you still here Mum? Do you like it? Don't you hate him?"

Paul hurled himself past the chairs and Laura's folder fell to the floor, scattering her drawings. Paul trampled over them, knocking a beer over in the process. Ria was crying and the last thing Sam saw was Babs looking at him, scared and humiliated, holding the green scarf to her neck. Everyone was on their feet and the tape kept on playing – was it a rerun of the same recording or further incidents – it was hard to tell in the commotion.

Sam ran from the house and didn't look back. He had no plan, no money, but he laughed hysterically as he sprinted, exhilarated, unburdened.

Chapter six

2021

Sam knelt beside the grave and touched the soft earth. He had no tears. He'd spent more than half his lifetime divorced from his relatives after his actions in 1996 when he effectively severed himself from the family unit. It was way too late for regrets, but he did want to just sit for a while, now the others had gone.

The wind was racing through the cemetery and he pulled up his coat around his neck. Ironic that it was this time of the year when she passed, just a week before Christmas.

"I thought it was you."

Sam started and looked up, then stood, embarrassed that he'd been caught.

"Long time, no see," said Laura, drily.

"Sorry, I…. I thought you'd all gone…."

"I've sent the others ahead. I thought I saw you over there, during the service," she gestured further along the grass, "I wanted to check."

"Oh," Sam stuck his hands in his pockets and hunched up his shoulders. "You're all grown up."

"Yeah, it happened suddenly when I was twelve," Laura replied tartly, "I hated you for a long time."

"Yeah, I'm not surprised. Sorry."

"Where did you go? Where've you been for the last twenty-five years?"

"Oh, here and there, you know," he shrugged.

They looked at one another, words not coming easily, then settled their stare back on the grave.

"I can't believe she stayed. Even after that Christmas."

"She loved him. She loved us – you too, even after …."

"I thought it was my job to save her, the eldest, the only son, you know…"

"You probably did. He was different, got better, got help. Michaela stepped in."

"Yeah?"

"He did love her, in his way. Everything changed though after you....did what you did. He got a bit more patient and kept his temper more, but he became so … mild. He wasn't Dad anymore. He lost all his charisma, all his charm. Broken…" Laura looked at Sam accusingly, "You did that."

"He looks old now, frail."

"He is. He's not well and he misses Mum."

They both looked at the mound of earth.

"I missed you all. I wasn't far away, you know. Sometimes I'd watch you and Ria coming and going. I was going to come back when she left him …"

"We never knew," Laura had tears in her eyes, "We missed you."

"Didn't anyone else ever know what was happening?"

"I heard them sometimes, mainly Dad's raised voice, but I

spent most of my time in my bedroom, didn't I, drawing? It made me wonder, after, about those times Dad came and sat on the floor of my bedroom... Ria was too young, I suppose – she says she never saw anything. I think Michaela suspected – she seemed the least surprised that night."

"I still don't get it. How could she still love him?"

"Didn't you love him?"

"Yes, when he was funny and loud, and cool with my friends. When he turned up at my matches."

"Well, Mum had times like that too. She told me afterward that she knew how much we all idolised him, how it warmed her heart to watch us all laughing together, being a family. Somehow, it made the darker times bearable."

Sam absorbed the information quietly. "I wish I'd seen her again, properly, to talk. I was so angry with her for putting up with it. Every time I thought about her, I'd be raging inside. And I was terrified I would become like him. And then too much time passed, and it was too late. I couldn't."

"Are you on your own? Do you have a family?"

"Yeah, I have a family. Wife. One kid. You?"

"Divorced. No kids."

"What happened to everyone else, after that night?"

"Well, we didn't have much of a Christmas!" Laura smiled, "Ria and I were bundled into the car and we all drove home in silence. My drawings were ruined but I took them home with me. When we got home, Mum took us inside and Dad drove off. We didn't see him til the next day.

Michaela and Mark came round on Boxing Day. Mark took us out and Michaela shut herself, Mum, and Dad in a room all day. They were great actually, Michaela and Mark – they were really there for us.

Holly walked, taking Timmy with her, saying our family was toxic and she didn't want Timmy to be anywhere near us. Poor Uncle Robert just buried himself in his work."

"Grandma and Grandpa?" prompted Sam.

Laura shook her head.

"What?"

"Dad was always her blue-eyed boy, wasn't he? What she heard on that tape broke her heart. She stopped eating and cried all the time. She just gave up. Three months later, she passed, Grandpa died too."

Sam dropped to his haunches and quietly wept. Laura crouched down and put her arms around him. There were no words.

"How will I know?" Sam sobbed, "How will I know I won't turn into him? What if I...."

"You won't," Laura soothed.

"Last night, at home, I came so close. I raised my hand .... I was so angry. She flinched, she was scared of me, and I saw Mum's face..."

"Sam, come back with me."

"I can't."

"'you won't just disappear again? Dad got help, maybe you

can. You need to move away from these memories, Sam. It sounds like you're stuck in 1996."

'I never meant to hurt you all. I never really thought about what would happen after, I just had to make it stop."

"I know. You're not him, Sam. But I do think you should talk to him. You'll find him changed, but he never stopped loving you. You made him face up to what he'd become and he knows that took guts. He respects you. He doesn't blame you. And he doesn't blame you about Grandma and Grandpa, he blames himself for that. Come back with me."

Laura helped Sam to his feet. They both gazed at the mound of earth and each heard their mother's voice saying, "Good. Now take care of one another, my darlings."

Taking each other's hands, they picked their way along the uneven ground to the path, and to a future with the possibility of hope and forgiveness.

Indigestion

The fog was getting thicker – a real pea-souper they'd have called it in the olden days. If that was the case then this would have been thick, pea and ham soup, dense as a brick with the occasional solid form to collide with, as Daniel had found to his painful expense when he stood on something on the lawn which had catapulted him through the air like an Olympic gymnast who fell short because of a failed landing. Daniel's body was long and lean, and his limbs even longer, and his control of them was clumsy at the best of times. Like a newborn giraffe, he would need to develop more finesse to avoid embarrassing mishaps if this was the career he would be taking up. It was fortunate that Daniel could not see the expression of contempt on the face of his accomplice as he hissed "Watch your step, you dimwit."

It was around 2 am and the occupant of the house should have been well asleep by now, but the light had lit up the bathroom, visible as a smudgy break in the fog, but making little impression on the visibility outdoors where the two men stood, ducking down beside the small wooden shed at the far end of the back garden. In front and to their side was an expanse of lawn which they would have to dart across to reach the rear entrance. It was impossible to see whether there were any more obstacles in the way such as gardening tools, garden furniture, or toys. Did the old girl have grandchildren? Perhaps he should have looked into that. Thankfully, there would be no dog to contend with on this job. Anthony took a moment to consider their next move. If it was daylight one would have noted that Anthony's lack of hair revealed a misshaped head with many protuberances that would have fascinated any phrenologist. The top of his head was flattened as if filed down so that if required, he could confidently bring you tea and toast on a tray balanced upon his head. Several scars marked the skin, cataloguing his life, some of them extending forward onto his face, straight lines which suggested that they had been made by the sharp edge of a blade. One would have supposed that such a person would have a nickname of 'Tramlines' or 'Bumphead' in the Dickensian manner of a name describing the character or role that character would play in the story, but Anthony had no such moniker. This misnomer, which evoked characteristics of hard work and good parenting, was the name by which all knew him, from the gangs on the street to the local constabulary.

Distracted by a noise coming from his right, he hissed at Daniel, "What are you doing?"

"Looking for my Gaviscon"

"What?!!"

"Gaviscon. I'm feeling a bit ropey" Daniel explained.

"I don't believe it," muttered Anthony.

"Oh, it's really good," whispered Daniel reassuringly. "It works a treat. It 'aids indigestion and heartburn.' I'm troubled with both from time to time, sometimes because of something I ate or if I'm feeling a bit stressed"

"Can't you just concentrate on what we're doing now, for Pete's sake"

"Oh, I'll be able to concentrate so much better when I have this" Daniel replied helpfully. "I had some cod and chips for my dinner and I don't think it's agreed with me. Here it is." Daniel took a slug, draining the last dregs out of the bottle.

"What's that?" Anthony jumped back a step, having felt something tapping against his feet. "I think there's a fox or a badger or something".

"No, it's just me." Daniel's voice seemed to be coming up from the ground. "I dropped the bottle and I'm trying to find it. I don't suppose I should be leaving it lying around. If it smashed, someone might stand on it and cut their foot".

"Not to mention they'd have DNA evidence to bring them straight to your door, you daft sod".

Now the two of them were scrambling on their knees on the grass, patting the ground with their hands and trying to locate the bottle. Eventually, the bottle found, they turned their attention back to their task.

"Right," said Anthony, "if you've finished messing around, I think it's time to make a move. I'll dash across the grass to the door, you count to 60 then follow me."

"Ok," whispered Daniel. "What if I can't find you?"

"What do you mean?"

"Well, you know the layout of the house and garden 'cause you've been here before, but I don't. I can't see the end of my arm, so how will I know which way you've gone?"

"Well you just saw the light, didn't you? Well, imagine the light is twelve o'clock, the back door is going to be about five to."

"What if I get there at ten to?"

"What?"

"Well, if it's five to from where you're standing, it might be ten to from where I'm standing. How will I find you?"

Anthony sighed. "I suppose I'll find you. Right, I'm going. Remember, count to 60, then you follow"

As Anthony set off, the ear-piercing scream of a siren from an ambulance or Police car broke through, raising the heart rate of both men.

On the other side of the garden, Anthony hissed "Where are you, man? Damn it, where've you gone?"

"I'm here, I'm here now," Daniel was breathless.

"Where've you been? That was more than 60 seconds."

"Yeah, I thought I'd wait 'til the noise of the siren died down, so I'd be able to hear you when I got here."

"The siren would have been a good cover for you running over here, you dumbbell. Right, so do you remember what you're looking for? Don't get distracted, we're here for one thing, and one thing only, and that's the ring. We get that and tick, job done and we're out of here, right?

"Rightio," said Daniel.

"Then we make a sharp exit, ok? Straight back the way we came, quick as a flash. By the way, what was that noise just then?"

"This noise?" The sound of tapping came again.

"Yeah, that. What is it?"

"It's the bottle banging against my keys when I move my leg."

"You and that blasted bottle! You're a liability! Move it to a different pocket, will you? You're gonna give the game away making all that racket. Who brings a bottle of Gaviscon on a job!!"

Anthony made a mental note to find a different partner for his next job. His stress levels were through the roof and they weren't even in the house yet. But he had chosen Daniel for his slim physique and now was when it was going to be put to good use.

"See down here, on the bottom door panel? I want you to climb through that dog flap …"

"I thought you said she didn't have a dog? I'm a bit nervous of dogs, Anthony. They don't seem to like me."

Anthony made fists with both hands and mentally counted to ten. "There. Is. No. Dog! Just climb through the dog flap and creep upstairs, remembering to step over the 7th one because that's the one that creaks, yeah? The old woman sleeps in the second bedroom on the right at the top of the stairs – she showed me that when I delivered her new telly last week. She said she wasn't getting the dog flap sealed until next month so that gives us a perfect opportunity to get the ring. She's deaf as a doorpost so you should be alright, so long as her daughter hasn't stayed over tonight. She keeps the ring on her bedside table near her glass of water, so be careful. I'll be waiting right here for you. I need you to crank it up now, mate. Get your act together and let's get this finished." Anthony gave Daniel a reassuring pat on his shoulder as he gently pressed him to his knees.

Daniel managed to slip through the dog flap without a sound. Anthony raised himself up and assessed the night. The fog looked like it was here to stay, so that should work in their favour as they left the property. He could hardly make out the fence separating the gardens so there was little chance of them being seen. Even if there was any CCTV anywhere, and he was pretty sure there wasn't, they wouldn't pick out their images in this. Surprisingly quickly, he felt the flap knock his leg as it opened and Daniel sloped out of the house.

"Did you get it?"

"Yeah. Easy. It was exactly where you said, and she was sending the cows home. Didn't even move. No sign of anyone else in the house."

"Brilliant. Right, let's go."

They made their way across the lawn, confidence rising now that they had their booty.

Back in the van, Anthony said, "Let's see it then."

"Oh yeah. "Daniel's chest puffed up with pride as he put his hand inside his sweatshirt pocket. "Hang on a minute." He felt in his other pocket, and then with mounting panic, in both trouser pockets.

"Where is it?" Anthony asked, his patience being stretched beyond its limits by now. "Where did you put it?"

"I had a great idea," said Daniel. "It was so small I was scared of losing it so I thought I could bung it in the medicine bottle, wrapped in a tissue. And 'cause you moaned about the bottle making a noise with my keys, I put it in my sweatshirt pocket. But it's not there now."

"Well, where is it, you muttonhead? You'd better not be having me on. I swear I'll kill you."

**

Early the next morning Nelly went downstairs in her dressing gown for breakfast. At the foot of the stairs, just in front of the old dog flap, she saw a Gaviscon bottle, with a tissue posted inside. Her stomach felt much more settled now. It had been a long while since her stomach had awakened her at night and she hoped last night wasn't signalling another bout of her indigestion. She hadn't remembered coming downstairs for the bottle but she had been so tired she accepted that perhaps she had – sometimes it was hard to differentiate between her dreams and reality. Feeling the vibration of the large refuse collection van through the floor she opened the door, taking the Gaviscon bottle with her. She dropped it into her dustbin and dragged it to the front of the house for the men to take away. As she looked down the street she noticed a van had crashed into the lamp post. The police were inspecting it and both doors were open but its occupants were gone. "It was probably that fog last night", she thought, looking up at the sky which was slowly returning to something resembling blue with the warmth of the sun. "I do hope they're alright and haven't injured themselves." Pulling her dressing gown around her, Nelly stepped back into her hallway and closed the door.

A recipe for love

Frank blamed the onions for the tears trickling down his wrinkled cheeks. Brushing them away roughly with the back of his hands, he continued to push the sharp knife through the firm vegetables, the blade hitting the glass cutting board and echoing through the kitchen. Sweeping the small pieces into the pan and cooking them slowly, he was comforted by the sound of them sizzling. He unpeeled the garlic, and squeezed the press, adding the mulch to the onions, giving them a quick stir with his wooden spoon. He shook his head as he remembered how he had been teased in the many kitchens he had worked for his bulging and malformed nose, resembling an overgrown garlic bulb.

Breaking the mince into the pan and stirring it into the onion mixture, his thoughts turned to that fateful evening thirty-five years ago – the last time he had seen his daughter. Carrie had celebrated her sixteenth birthday a month earlier and they'd agreed that she could work in the restaurant and receive a small wage. Frank and Marjorie were increasingly concerned about the company Carrie was keeping, kids who spent more time out of school than in, who hung around the streets in gangs, taunting and intimidating the adults who passed by. Giving her something productive to do with her time, along with some responsibility, could be the making of her, getting some sense into her before the rot set in. Carrie had been keen to start, proved to be punctual and helpful, not afraid of the hard work involved in running a busy establishment.

Tipping the tomatoes into the pan and adding the stock, Frank stirred. He felt the nausea rise as he remembered what he had seen towards the end of that fateful evening. The kitchen door had swung open as a waitress returned some empty crockery and Frank had turned his head at the exact moment that Carrie had removed some money from the till, dropping it into her little apron, looking around her to ensure that she'd not been observed. She'd chosen a moment when the bar staff and fellow waiting staff were busily occupied, probably not realising that she could be seen from the kitchen. Frank had been stunned. Shocked at the actions of his daughter, stealing from her own father, he had been uncertain of what to do. Unable to challenge her whilst there were customers to serve, he would need to confront her when they got home. The evening had stretched on interminably until he closed the restaurant at almost midnight.

Frank was not a man to avoid any necessary conflict. He didn't seek out trouble, indeed he would make every attempt to prevent situations that would cause any upset, but when required, he could be direct and do what was necessary – "Frank by name and Frank by nature" his wife would say. But to be betrayed by someone he loved! He couldn't bear to break Marjorie's heart and resolved to tackle Carrie immediately, putting an end to this nonsense before it spiralled out of control.

Taking the slab of cold cheese, he began to grate it, sliding the block across the punctured metal, watching the strings of cheese emerge. He wondered as he had so many times, whether he could have handled things differently. When he got home it was late and Carrie was in her bedroom. He'd climbed the stairs and knocked on Carrie's door, half hoping she'd gone to sleep, that he wouldn't need to face his daughter and tell her that he'd witnessed her theft, but instead he heard her call, "Come in."

She was sitting cross-legged on her bed, earphones on. Frank asked her to remove them. He didn't sit alongside her on the bed as he would normally have done. Instead, he remained standing, just inside the door.

"I saw what you did tonight."

Carrie looked at him, uncomprehending.

"Well, what have you got to say for yourself?"

"I don't know what you mean." She replied, hesitantly.

"I think you do, Carrie. I think you know exactly what I mean. Was it the first time, tonight? Or have you stolen from the till before?"

Carrie said nothing. She stared back at him, her jaw set tight, her eyes like flint. Frank hardly recognised his sweet daughter in the hard face returning his stare.

"What's happened to you? I don't know you anymore! What kind of daughter steals from her own family? After everything we've done for you." Frank could feel his voice rising as the hurt and disappointment overcame him. "Well, don't you have anything to say for yourself, girl?" He yelled.

Carrie remained silent, her body language unrepentant. Frank thought he detected hatred in her eyes and then he said it – the words he would regret for the rest of his life.

"You are no daughter of mine when you behave like this. We're finished – do you hear? Finished! I don't want to see you, I don't want to hear anything from you until you are ready to apologise."

Turning his back to her, he marched from her room. The next morning, she was gone.

This time Frank could not blame the onions for the tears that escaped as he began to make the roux for the bechamel sauce. He stirred the flour and butter into a paste and gradually added milk to the pan, mixing all the time, stirring round and round as if by doing so he could turn back the clock to that pivotal night, altering the course of the life of his family.

He never told Marjorie. For thirty-five years the last

conversation he had with his daughter had remained a secret. He couldn't bear for Marjorie to know that it was his fault that Carrie had left home. He was responsible for their estrangement. He'd destroyed his small family by his words, words that he'd wished he could retract every hour of every day since.

With the addition of the cheese, the sauce began to thicken and Frank dared to hope that this meal would be a sort of glue that would stick his family together again. Lasagne had always been Carrie's favourite when she was a girl. He wanted to show her that he remembered, that he loved her still.

The letter had arrived last week, addressed to him in familiar handwriting. When he saw the envelope his stomach had performed a loop. He'd glanced up at Marjorie seated on the recliner chair to his right, short and stout, small rivulets of water running down large lymphatic legs. She had lost her best years to grief. Years when she should have enjoyed an adult relationship with her daughter, perhaps become a grandmother. He'd stolen those years from her, a much worse crime than Carrie had committed when stealing a few pounds from the till. Offering to make a cup of tea, Frank slipped the letter into his trouser pocket and read it privately.

"Hi, Dad,

It's me. I hope you and mum are ok.

I wanted to say I'm sorry. I'd like to see you. Can you email me? Please?

Carrie****@gmail.com

Love,

Carrie"

Frank had read the words over and over. Carrie wanted to

see them! She had been in touch after all this time. After several years of fruitless searching, he and Marjorie had resigned themselves that she no longer wanted any contact. They'd remained hopeful that she was still alive and one day would get in touch. And now she had! Frank turned on his laptop immediately.

"Carrie,

My darling girl. Is that really you? How are you? Are you well?

I can't tell you how glad I am to hear from you! Of course, we want to see you. We've never stopped loving you. We've missed you so much. Where have you been all these years? We have so many questions, but that can wait.

Come home, love. Please, come home.

Your loving Dad."

In recent days emails had passed between father and daughter. Carrie had not shared much of her life, just that she wanted to make amends, that she was sorry. Frank invited her to come for Sunday lunch – tempting her with her favourite - lasagne.

Placing the lasagne in the oven, Frank began to set the table. She was due in 15 minutes. He could hardly believe it. What would Marjorie say? What a wonderful surprise this would be! His heart felt like it would burst. A chance for redemption, perhaps he could even tell Marjorie about that terrible evening all those years ago, now Carrie was back. They would be a family again. He popped through to the living room to tell Marjorie, dozing in her chair, that the meal would soon be ready. He looked at his wife of 55 years – he loved her with all his heart. They had struggled with fertility, having one child, only to lose her after such a short time. The photographs on display around the room showed Carrie as a baby, a toddler, and a young woman still to grow into full maturity. Then there was a full stop – no photographs of graduation, or marriage; no images of grandchildren or happy holidays. In many ways, their life had paused after Carrie left. Unable to move to another property in the vague hope that one day the doorbell would ring and they would find Carrie on the doorstep, her room remained unchanged. Frank gently tapped his wife's arm.

"Almost ready, love. I'll just put the plates in to warm."

He glanced at the clock – she should be here any time. He lifted three plates from the cupboard and placed them in the oven; as he closed the door he heard his phone ping. Taking the mobile from his pocket he unlocked the screen, seeing the words

"I'm sorry dad. I can't do it. I'm not ready. I'm so sorry."

With a heavy heart, he typed "Alright love. No rush. There's plenty of time. Whenever you're ready, we'll be here."

Walking back to the oven he removed one of the plates and returned it to the cupboard. In the dining room, he removed the third place setting and glass.

When the meal was ready, Marjorie joined him and they ate in companionable silence, each with their own thoughts.

"You went to town today, love. You've made enough to feed the five thousand!"

"I know, Pet," Frank replied, "I must have slipped back into the old days for a minute. It'll keep. We'll have something on standby, in case we have visitors."

"Visitors!" Marjorie retorted, "Whoever would be visiting us!"

"You never know," Frank responded, his heart full of hope, "Perhaps one day."

Aisle 36

"I'm in Aisle 36," I type.

My hands are shaking as I replace my flip-top phone in the front pocket of my bag. I've done it. I can hardly breathe. I recognise the agonising indecision I always felt at school – would I just laugh the bullying off and pretend I didn't care? Should I speak to my parents or one of my teachers? Dare I actually stand up to this girl, with her loud voice and sniggering friends?

The screech of a young child makes me jump, the high-pitched yell drowning out the beeps of people self-scanning items and bagging their shopping as they made their way around the store.

I steal a furtive glance to my side as somebody appears around the corner but no, it's not her. The supermarket is huge - it may take several minutes before I come face to face with her for the first time in thirty-six years. Will she even recognise me? People change, don't they? Although, as I think about my own appearance, I still wear my hair at a similar length and style as I had as a teenager. True, I have put on a few stones, but I feel confident that others can recognise me easily. Most relevantly for today, there are no obvious changes to my distinctive teeth! I shudder as I hear the taunts again – 'Alright, Mister Ed?' – followed by the scornful laughs from the hangers-on. I touch my lips subconsciously. As an adult I have received many compliments about my smile – 'You have such a beautiful smile,' 'What lovely teeth'...... and yet the comments that made the most lasting impact were those comparisons to the fictional TV horse. Children can be so cruel.

I've never felt confident, though I don't know why. I have vague memories of being chased by a gang of children at Primary School, of fights in the park that did not end well for me. There are no memories of physical altercations in Secondary School – just those jeers, usually led by one person. The tormentor was a heavy-set girl with big legs beneath her regulation-grey school skirt, folded over at the waistband to bring it a few inches shorter. We were in different classes, so there was some respite during the day, but before and after school, and at breaks, I would cautiously look around me, bracing myself for the brash voice that I was involuntarily tuned in to. I shiver – how can even the memory of that voice continue to have such power over me?

"Pull yourself together," I mutter under my breath. "You are the mother of two young adults, you've had a successful career. You have nothing to fear."

Time seemed to be passing as slowly as a cloud in a windless sky.

I remember the 'School Reunion' I attended years ago. I'd travelled alone on public transport after much consideration about the advantages and disadvantages of attending. I was keen to meet up with old school friends and curious about how their lives had unfolded. I couldn't help but be intrigued to see if the school 'beauties' had retained their good looks. But as the bus had lumbered on towards the city centre, that voice and those taunts had begun to replay in my head, causing my pulse to rise and my hands to become clammy. I had entered the venue with some trepidation but my old friends had spotted me and called me over to join them, and I felt my body begin to relax. It was much later in the evening that a friend gestured to the other side of the room towards a slim woman with dyed blond hair and a face full of heavy make-up.

"Do you see who's here?"

I studied the woman, not immediately able to put a name to the face, but then heard the voice rise above the chatter. Instinctively, I brought my hand to my mouth, a chill making its way along the length of my spine. The voice had not changed, though the face and body had, considerably.

My friends looped their hands under my arms and ushered me toward the buffet table. I spent the rest of the evening avoiding my tormentor in the attentive protection of those who cared for me.

And now, after all these years, here I am, in Aisle 36, waiting to meet the person I've spent most of my life trying to avoid and forget.

Was this a terrible mistake? A trap? An opportunity to exert power one last time?

"I must be crazy!" I think.

A young boy runs down the aisle, ricocheting from shelf to shelf like an unbroken horse at a rodeo, pursued by his mother, who looked both exhausted and defeated. I give a sympathetic smile to the downtrodden woman, which was received with a scowl.

I was astonished when an old school friend telephoned last week saying that Susan had been in touch and wanted to meet up with me.

"No way!" I said, remembering how Susan had robbed me of confidence and happiness for many years.

"I think she's changed," the friend ventured.

"Humph, I'll believe that when I see it."

"Meet with her then!"

"Are you some kind of sadist? Don't you remember how she always made me feel? What does she even want?"

"I don't know. But she went to an awful lot of trouble to get my number."

I considered the request.

"Well, it needs to be somewhere public and somewhere I can escape from easily without a scene if she starts any of her antics."

"That does make sense," my friend agreed. "A coffee shop?"

"No, if she does start with her old tricks I don't want people to hear her and I don't want to feel cornered. The supermarket." I said decisively.

"The supermarket? Okay, I see what you mean. Which one and when?"

And now I am about to meet with my nemesis. I even dug out my old 'Pay as you go' phone to avoid giving my mobile number away in case it all went terribly wrong.

As I gaze down Aisle 36 I see a woman begin to walk toward me. The woman isn't carrying a basket or pushing a trolley. She wears practical, black shoes over broad feet topped with thick ankles. The hair is still lightened but is no longer so blonde and the face wears only a thin application of foundation and mascara. An uncertain smile flickers across her lips, and I find myself reciprocating.

"Thank you for meeting me."

"I was surprised you wanted to."

"Yes, well, I've been doing a lot of thinking lately."

"Thinking about what?"

"You. Me. School. How I treated you. I wanted to apologise."

I feel my knees weaken. My heart races and I feel slightly light-headed. I don't know what to say.

"I was horrible to you. I don't even know why really. I suppose you were an easy target and it made me feel good."

Tears begin to prick my eyes.

"There's no real excuse. I shouldn't have done it. You didn't deserve it. I'm sorry."

Susan's voice has lost its harshness. The apology sounds genuine.

"'t's ok," I reply, feeling confused and uncomfortable.

"No, it's not. It's not ok. I was a bully to you. The things I said. How it must have made you feel." Susan's eyes never leave mine. Her eyes are pleading, honest and remorseful, but she is facing her shame head-on. "You could have done anything."

Puzzled, I frown. Susan's eyes fill with tears.

"I've seen the other side of it now. I know the damage it can do. My daughter was bullied a bit at school, but then it carried on into uni. She…. she killed herself. Took tablets and left a note saying sorry, but she couldn't carry on."

My hand has unconsciously reached out to Susan's arm.

"I'm so sorry."

"Some might say it was poetic justice. What goes around comes around. But she didn't deserve it. She was just a young girl with all her life ahead of her. She was beautiful."

I feel my body relax. I realise that I've been holding tension for years as if clinging to the edge of a cliff, terrified of the fall. My unlikely rescuer has been the very perpetrator who tipped me over the edge in the first place. I no longer need to cling –I can relax my fingers, and loosen my grip. I have been freed!

"Let's go and get a coffee," I offer to the broken woman before me.

"Really? I *am* sorry you know. I hope you can forgive me."

"I can," I reply, placing my arm around the shoulder of my old attacker, "I do."

Digging deeper

There was something of Rasputin about him, with his long, unwashed hair and his grey-flecked beard. His mouth was almost completely hidden by the voluminous growth, just a small section of the soft, pink lower lip in evidence. Some of the longer hairs in his eyebrows formed a curtain over his eyes.

Every feature of hers was tiny – small, beady eyes, a nose that barely protruded from her face, and thin lips which seemed reluctant to stretch into a smile, preferring to remain pursed together as if held there by blanket stitch. Her thin hair was scraped off her face into a tight bun on the back of her head, very few strands managing to escape their tethering, even as the strong wind whipped around them.

The wind had been steadily gathering speed across the open moorland, but thankfully the dark brooding clouds had not yet disgorged their contents. Edward raised his eyes skyward, weighing the likelihood of a sudden drenching against the sinister company of the two people standing before him. No sign of the skylarks which had been singing enthusiastically, and even the buzzards and harriers which had been soaring above had now disappeared, choosing shelter as a better option.

Looking down at his ten-year-old son, he said, "Your mother'll kill me, Kenny, if you get sick and have to miss school. It'll be the end of our treasure hunting, that's for sure."

Kenny shivered in his thin jumper and jeans, his headset hanging around his neck and his metal detector in his hands. Edward cursed under his breath as he remembered the hat and warm coat sitting on the back seat of his car, forgotten in the excitement of the quest. Looking across at the unfriendly couple, and the stone cottage behind them with smoke rising from the single chimney, Edward decided that they must seek shelter for an hour or two, giving the storm time to pass. It would be impossible to get back to the car before the heavens opened and he was feeling pretty cold himself, his coat being alongside Kenny's in the car park. Adjusting the straps of his rucksack and hoisting his spade over his shoulder, he led the way forward, lifting his hand in greeting.

"Hi, hello there," he shouted across the sound of the wind, "boy, are we glad to see you! We've been out for a few hours but weren't prepared for this weather. Left our coats in the car in all our excitement to get out on our treasure hunt!"

Edward thought he saw an eyebrow twitch on 'Rasputin's' face, but otherwise, their expressions remained rigid. Feeling uncomfortable, he held out his hand,

"Edward, and this is my son, Kenny."

After a few awkward seconds, during which the couple silently stared at the boy, they turned with a barely perceptible nod and headed towards the cottage. Kenny looked questioningly at his father and Edward gave him an exaggerated grin of encouragement which suggested far greater confidence in the situation than he actually felt.

They entered the door and the warmth enveloped them as they moved into the tiny space toward the log fire. The smell of the wood as it burned and the flickering flames were hypnotic. Edward and Kenny took the only two seats at the silent invitation of the woman. They both jumped when the bark cracked and popped as it burned, then giggled together in relief. The woman took a heavy iron kettle from the fire and proceeded to prepare a hot drink for them both.

Edward looked around him at the exposed brick walls and low beams. Although still only early afternoon the cottage was dark, a single candle flickering on a rustic table, tiny windows with even smaller square panes of glass, a couple of them cracked. The chairs they were sitting in were low and Edward could see bits of what looked like horsehair emerging from holes in the upholstery. 'Rasputin' and his wife were whispering at the other end of the room, with occasional glances towards the boy. Kenny was studying the silver belt buckle he had just unearthed, his imagination fired by the possibilities of who this had belonged to. Edward suspected it wasn't very old – they hadn't had to dig very deep for it and the soil had brushed off it without much effort. It was possible that it had been unearthed by a dog and then reburied but it was probably no older than Kenny. Still, it had brought his son some pleasure and it was something he would enjoy showing at the 'Young Archeologists' club next time.

Steaming cups of liquid were handed to Edward and Kenny, and Edward smiled as he saw his son's reaction. He was proud as Kenny looked at the woman and thanked her politely, before looking at his father questioningly. The biscuit that was then supplied was greeted with much more enthusiasm and hungrily consumed immediately. The woman seemed to have taken root beside Kenny's chair and watched him intently, the expression on her face impassive. 'Rasputin' had disappeared. With the hot liquid warming him and being soothed by the flames, Edward felt his eyes grow heavy.

*

"And this is a coin I found." Kenny said proudly.

When Edward opened his eyes he panicked for a moment – where was he? Yes, the old cottage with the strange couple. Was Kenny ok? How had he allowed himself to fall asleep? Stupid idiot! Lorraine would kill him if she knew. He turned to the sound of Kenny's voice.

Kenny was standing at the wooden table and had tipped all the findings of the day out of the rucksack. There were a couple of modern 5p coins and an old 1992 10p coin, a toy car (Edward intended to check if it was an old Matchbox car that could be worth serious money), the sliver buckle, and several pull tabs off cans found together that were probably the detritus left by teenage boys on a drinking spree. 'Rasputin' eyed the treasure curiously, particularly the silver buckle, and his wife appeared to be hanging on every word that Kenny spoke. Kenny seemed completely at ease with them and Edward began to relax as he listened.

"My Dad got me the metal detector for my birthday. This is only the third time we've used it and we've found loads of stuff already. It's in my bedroom at home. Sometimes I take things to school to show my class or take it to the 'Young Archeologists' club. I like to make stories up about who owned the things before they were lost. One day, I hope to find a whole chest of Roman coins or something – that would be so cool."

Edward rose to his feet and stretched, then walked towards the group and peered out of the window. There was no evidence of the storm now, the sky was blue and the sun was shining brightly.

"Right, kiddo, I think we should leave these good people in peace now." Turning to face 'Rasputin' Edward held out his hand as he said, "Thank you so much. You saved our lives there! His mother would never let me forget it if she knew we'd come up here without our coats and hats!"

His hand was not taken, but 'Rasputin' gave a barely perceptible nod. His wife looked slightly alarmed and shot a glance to Kenny and then to her husband. Edward scooped the 'treasure' back into the rucksack and swung it on his shoulder. Collecting the spade from the back door and putting a hand protectively on Kenny's shoulder, he ushered him towards the door.

"Well, thanks again," he said.

"Thank you," called Kenny with a broad smile.

Edward was keen to put some distance between them and the cottage as soon as possible and struck a fast pace, Kenny needing to jog along beside him. Checking his watch, he saw it was now four-thirty and they should return to the car as quickly as possible.

"They were a strange couple, weren't they, Dad?" Kenny said, slightly breathless from his jogging.

"Mad as a box of frogs if you ask me," Edward replied. "I can't believe I fell asleep and left you with them. Don't tell your Mum, will you?"

"They were ok", Kenny smiled. "'hey didn't seem scary, just a bit weird. They just kept staring at me, especially the lady. That's why I started to show them my stuff."

"Well, at least they saved us from the rain, eh," Edward said, tousling his son's blonde curls.

*

It was three days later when Edward dropped Kenny off for the 'Young Archeologists' club at the Local History Museum. Enjoying his customary cup of coffee in the café while waiting for the club to finish, Edward noticed that a new display had been mounted on the walls featuring photographs and newspaper cuttings, as well as hand-written contributions from local people, sharing their stories. Carrying his coffee, he moved closer to look and his eyes were immediately drawn to a black and white photograph from an old newspaper from 1932.

"Boy's parents now missing too. Feared lost on the moorlands."

Staring out from the photograph were the faces of 'Rasputin' and his wife, impassive, inscrutable. They were dressed exactly as they had been when they invited Edward and Kenny into their shelter. Edward hadn't given any thought to how they had dressed but now remembered she had worn a dress to her calf with a full-length white apron over the top, and 'Rasputin' had worn a scratchy jacket with a waistcoat beneath, and a woollen flat cap atop his head. He read the article with a faint trickle of sweat creeping over his skin.

"The parents of Kenneth Taylor have not been seen for three weeks, say locals. The family lived quietly in a small cottage on the open moorland, their nearest neighbonour being a good hour's ride away. They had little contact with the outside world and it is believed that their son was born late in their marriage. Kenneth's attendance at school was sporadic and it was thought that he spent most of his time roaming the moorlands while his parents worked their small farm. It is now six months since he went missing and his parents have regularly been seen scouring the countryside for him. Locals have noticed that they have more recently taken to standing outside their cottage for long hours, staring into the distance, still hoping to see their boy. It is thought that the whole family is now lost. Police will continue to search the countryside for their bodies."

Below the article was a photograph of a young boy, aged about ten, with longish, blonde curly hair. His resemblance to Kenny was striking. Edward's head was spinning. How could this be? He looked again at the grainy photograph of the couple. 'Rasputin's' jacket was open and his waistcoat was a little too short on his long frame. The buckle of his trousers glinted as the camera flash caught it and Edward noticed the silver buckle that Kenny had unearthed that afternoon, just before the storm had arrived.

Going Under

His voice had that slightly husky, higher note that many Scotsmen have, and his accent rose and fell with a musical cadence that was pleasing to the ear. She'd always loved to listen to him, never tired of his stories, never grown bored because he made her laugh with his silly asides and corny jokes. She missed that most of all. His wit. How long had it been now, since they'd laughed together?

Veronica sighed and glanced over at her husband, dozing in the armchair, long legs crossed and arms folded onto his stomach. She knew she should be relaxing, taking this opportunity to rest and recuperate, because once he awoke it would all start again. The endless pacing, the restlessness which would lead to yet another struggle as he tried to leave the house and she would have to prevent this from happening. She'd somehow found herself cast as the enemy, confining Ken to their home against his wishes. There would be raised voices again, perhaps even a raised fist.

The first time Ken had raised his fist to her she'd been shocked. He was not the man she had loved for 51 years. Her Ken was gentle, and patient, and had never shown a hint of violence in all their life together. 'The Professionals' were sympathetic but forthright – 'It's his frustration, you see. Ken can't process the things going on around him anymore. He will be confused, disoriented, frightened....' Well, what about her? She was frightened too – frightened of this disease that was obliterating the man she loved; frightened that he would hurt her; frightened that she had to face this alone without his support. She was also frightened that she might have stopped loving him.

Veronica's attention was drawn back to the television as

the presenter chatted to Captain Tom Moore about his sponsored walk. She listened as the old gentleman, proudly wearing his medals across his left breast pocket, spoke, 'We will get through it in the end but it might take time, but at the end of the day it will all be ok again…. the sun will shine on you again and the clouds will go away.'

Veronica wiped a tear from her cheek. "No offence, Captain Tom, you're a lovely man but I can't agree with you on that one."

Ken stirred in his chair and Veronica braced herself. She felt like she was always on edge, ever alert to Ken's moods and movements. Neither had slept much last night as Ken patrolled the house, checking and rechecking the doors and windows were locked, over and over and over. She had started to keep the landing and bathroom lights on to help Ken find the toilet during the night, but this meant that the house was never in darkness, so Ken couldn't understand that it was time to sleep. They no longer had conversations; sometimes he would say just a few words and she would have to guess what it was that he wanted or needed. If she guessed wrong, the fist would come up and she would flinch from the man she had vowed to love in sickness and health.

Before the Pandemic, the day would have been broken up a little by a walk along the canal, a cup of tea in town, or perhaps an hour of people-watching while sitting on a bench in the park. Ken would be able to walk off his restlessness somewhat and then settle in his chair for a nap. But now the country was in complete lockdown.

"The single most important action we can all take in fighting Coronavirus is to stay at home…" said the Prime Minister, "People may only leave home to exercise for one hour a day."

Veronica had listened to the announcement with horror and dread. Didn't they understand? How could she keep Ken confined to the house for 23 hours a day? How could she possibly make him understand? And how long was this going to last? She had never felt more alone than in recent weeks.

Ken's eyes opened and he looked around, trying to place himself. Veronica felt herself stiffen as she assessed his mood. His fingers began to drum on the arm of his chair and he uncrossed his legs. He stood suddenly, overbalancing slightly and having to take a couple of sidesteps to regain his stability.

"What is it, Love?" Veronica asked.

"Must get home…" Ken mumbled.

"It's alright, Ken, you're already at home. This is your home." Veronica rose to her feet.

"No, no, I need to get home now." Ken began to walk towards the front door.

"You can't go out, Ken. You have to stay here."

Ken ignored her and turned the handle of the door. Thankfully, she had remembered to lock it and wore the key around her neck on a chain, underneath her clothes. Finding the door locked, Ken began tapping his trouser pockets, trying to locate his keys.

"Come on, love. Let's watch a bit of telly."

"No, I'm going home."

Veronica reached forward to take Ken's arm, hoping to guide him to the sitting room, but he shrugged her off and strode past her towards the kitchen. She followed him, remembering the biscuits she had made earlier, cooling on the tray. Perhaps these would serve as a distraction. That's what 'The Professionals' said, wasn't it? 'Don't contradict – distract!'

"I've made your favourite biscuits, Ken, look!"

She offered one of the biscuits to her husband but he pushed her arm away roughly and she dropped the biscuit, which Ken then trod into the tiled floor.

Veronica opened the fridge door and brought out a cold beer – never mind that it was only 11 am – she no longer cared. Confined to the home for 23 hours a day with a man living with dementia, who neither recognised her nor their home, had meant that the time of the day was increasingly irrelevant. What did it matter if it was 11 am or 11 pm – the hours would drag by just as slowly and they would go for days without speaking to another soul. Even the one-hour permitted exercise had brought no relief as Ken would not wear a face mask and had no understanding of social distancing. He'd approach dog walkers in the park and attempt to pat the dogs, and people had been incensed that he'd invaded their personal space, shouting at him angrily. Her apologies and explanations had fallen on deaf ears during these times of heightened anxiety. Being forced to take their walks in more secluded environments, and at times when fewer people were out, had only served to increase her sense of isolation.

The beer seemed to do the trick and Ken settled back in his chair. Veronica decided to wash her hair in an attempt to make herself feel better. Coming back downstairs, she began to prepare some sandwiches for lunch and put the radio on. She was humming along with Rod Stewart when she felt his arms slide around her waist.

"You're in my heart, you're in my soul," Ken sang into her hair, swaying her side to side, "You are my lover, you're my best friend..."

Veronica placed the knife on the worktop and turned in his arms, enjoying this precious moment of Ken knowing her, of being in the present, for however long it would last. They shuffled side to side, bodies held close, lost in the moment together. The song finished and Ken planted a kiss on her forehead before saying

"Well, I must be off now..."

Veronica's heart sank – Ground-hog day.

"You're home, Ken, here with me."

Ken ignored her, turning to leave the kitchen. She grabbed his arm and he pushed her violently. Losing her footing, she landed heavily on the hard tiles and her hip exploded with pain. Ken lifted the knife and pointed it at her.

"Don't you try to stop me!"

He left the room, taking the knife with him. Veronica struggled to her feet. 'Don't let him see you upset' 'The Professionals' had said, 'It'll confuse him; upset him. You need to make him feel safe.'

Taking the key from the teapot on the shelf, she unlocked the door to the garage and stepped into the cool air. Leaning against the wall she allowed her tears to fall. Just breathe, she thought. Just take ten minutes to yourself and breathe. Her hip was throbbing with pain but thankfully, no broken bones. Probably an enormous bruise tomorrow morning though, she thought grimly. It was difficult for her to guess how long she remained in the garage, no matter how often she was asked that question later, but eventually, she felt calm enough to return to the kitchen. The half-made sandwiches were drying out on the worktop, the knife was gone and so was Ken.

"Ken," she shouted, "where are you, Ken?"

Turning into the hallway, her stomach dropped – the front door was wide open. She ran upstairs, checked every room, and then ran out into the street.

"Ken!' Ken!"

The street was deserted, the roads empty. Driven by instinct, she ran towards the main road, calling Ken's name as she went. At the main road, she could see further but could not spot Ken. With rising panic, she turned back to the house.

"Is everything ok?" asked a neighbour, peeking out from behind her front door.

"No. It's Ken. He's got out. He's on his own and I don't know where he is."

"Have you rung the Police?"

"Not yet, no. I'll do that now," she said, taking her mobile out of her pocket.

It took about fifteen minutes for the police to arrive at her doorstep.

"Can you give us a description of Ken, Veronica?"

"Tall, silver hair, worn slightly long. He has dementia, he won't be able to find his way home. Please find him." Veronica gripped the arm of the young officer, forgetting about the Pandemic protocol.

"Tell us exactly what happened."

"He's always so restless, you see. Wants to go out, doesn't think he lives here. It's always causing arguments. I have to keep all the doors locked to keep him safe. I wear the key around my neck on a chain, but I washed my hair…. I took the chain off while I used my hairdryer, otherwise it gets hot and burns my neck. I must have forgotten to put it back on. I'm so tired. You do see, don't you? Oh, it's my fault. Do you think he'll be alright? Will you find him?"

"We'll get people out straight away, Veronica. Try not to worry," the female officer said. She had beautiful eyes, very brown, like chocolate buttons, and perfectly shaped eyebrows in a natural way. Veronica wondered at how peoples' eyes were so much more noticeable in these days of covering up much of the rest of the face. She was pleased that this pleasant girl was staying with her while the young man left to search for Ken. Veronica wrote down any places she could think of that Ken might try to get to – old addresses, favourite walks, etc.

The pretty-eyed policewoman picked up photo frames, admiring the pictures on display. Ken's 70th birthday and their golden wedding anniversary. The difference in Ken could be seen even then – his face a little thinner, his eyes indicating that his mind was elsewhere. The girl was a good listener. Veronica told her how they had met in their twenties, how Ken had charmed her with his wit and 'exotic' Scottish accent. She described their early courting days, acknowledging how different it is today.

"I feel sorry for young people today, Suzy. How are you supposed to meet someone when everyone is wearing these face masks? And only for one hour a day as well!"

Veronica threw away the dried-up bread and made some fresh sandwiches which they ate together, followed by her delicious biscuits. Though still concerned about Ken's welfare, she had to admit that she enjoyed Suzy's company and the chance for conversation. The time passed quite pleasantly, all things considered!

Some hours later, there was a knock on the door. Veronica was faced with a young boy, his bike lying across the path, the wheel still spinning, as if he had jumped off before stopping.

"It's Ken!" he said, breathlessly.

"Ken? Have you seen him?"

"Yes, my friends are still with him. He's by the canal. I think he's hurt himself – he can't stand up."

"How did you know he lived here?" asked Suzy, joining them at the door.

"I've seen you sometimes when you go out for a walk. I sit in my bedroom trying to write songs – I'm in a band," he shrugged, "I heard him shouting at you the other day. I just live over there."

The boy pointed to a house on the opposite side of the road, a little further down the street. He looked embarrassed. "I was worried about you so I watched you until you went into the house. My mum and dad keep a watch on you as well."

Suzy was on her radio and asked the boy to show her where Ken was.

"What's your name?"

"Carl." He said, lifting his bike from the floor and following

Suzy up the path.

Veronica gathered Ken's coat and some other essentials and gave them to Suzy, then waited for her to return.

*

Ken was brought home by ambulance the next morning, his right foot in plaster. Other than that, he wasn't any the worse for his adventure! He had no recollection of his accident and it would always remain a mystery how he had injured himself. When Carl's parents saw the ambulance arrive, they brought a wheelchair to Veronica and suggested she used it for Ken for as long as she needed it. It had been used by Carl's grandfather but was no longer required.

"He had dementia too," Carl's mother said quietly, and the two women exchanged a meaningful look.

Veronica settled Ken into his armchair and soon his eyes closed, exhausted by the events of the last 24 hours. Surprisingly, Veronica felt the opposite! Discovering that she was not alone after all had brought a new sense of purpose and renewed energy.

Holding her bruised hip, she rose to her feet, leaving Ken to sleep. Tapping her chest gently she reassured herself that the key was where it should be.

"Now," she said, turning on the oven to warm, "I must get on with those biscuits. I'll need one boxful to take down to the police station for Suzy and her colleagues to say thank you. Then another box for Carl's mum and dad – fancy them keeping an eye out for me and I didn't even know! Then I'll need to do an extra-large box for Carl and his friends – after all, they're growing boys!"

she chuckled to herself.

Having already decided that delivering these would bring purpose to their walks for the next three days, she was happy to see what would unfold after that......

Introspection

"Tokyo? By tomorrow? Just like that?"

"Yes, our flights at 7.30 pm" beamed Frannie, "Seize the day!"

"But why so suddenly?" asked Alana, staring at her twin sister in astonishment. "You've never mentioned this before. Where's this come from?"

"Oh, you know me," Frannie shrugged, "I always like to keep you guys on your toes. Si suggested it to me a couple of weeks ago, and I thought, why not". Frannie looked at the young man leaning against the living room wall with folded arms and Alana thought she saw something unspoken pass between them, just for a second, as if her normally self-assured, audacious sister was less certain in herself than she was willing to admit. Alana allowed her gaze to rest a little on Simon, who was watchful of Frannie, like a parent watching their child in a school nativity, inwardly mouthing the well-practiced script with them.

Simon had studied Game Design alongside Frannie, and although he had been pointed out by her sister at occasional events, he had not generally mixed in the same circles. Alana suspected that Frannie had always had a bit of a crush on this tall, good-looking man with his perfect honey brown skin and beautiful smile. Frannie was used to getting what she wanted – she'd always been the gifted one, able to control people and shape them in her hands like clay, whereas Alana had always been the less beautiful one of the two, the slightly muted shadow of her twin. Alana had never resented this and adored Frannie, luxuriating in the light reflected from her and enjoying watching how much her sister was admired by all.

Now Frannie turned to head to the bedroom to pack her bags and took Alana's hand as she passed.

"Come and talk to me while I pack," she said, ignoring a slight frown on Simon's face, "We won't be long. Don't worry, Si, she won't talk me out of it!"

Upstairs, Frannie pulled down her rucksack from the top of the wardrobe and flung it onto her bed. She began grabbing clothes indiscriminately, with little consideration for weather conditions or if they matched, unusual for her. Alana watched her, mind still reeling with the force that was her sister. She had always been impulsive, with little thought for the consequences of her actions, and Alana knew that her parents had spent many troubled nights thinking about their youngest daughter. It had been Frannie's recklessness, rather than Alana's seniority of 7 minutes that had probably caused her to become the 'ying' to Frannie's 'yang', balancing the chaos by her orderliness.

"Pass me that will you?" Frannie gestured to her oversized bag at the bottom of the bed.

Alana handed the bag to her twin and watched her take out an unfamiliar mini laptop, and then dig around searching for something, before withdrawing her hand which held a bunch of flash drives. Frannie looked at them for a second, glanced quickly at her sister, and then dropped them into her rucksack. She brought out loose sheets of paper on which Alana could see complicated diagrams and text – she had seen similar many times during their time at university, as Frannie had completed projects in her design course.

"Are you planning to do some work while you're travelling then?" she asked, nodding to the rucksack.

"Yeah. Well, that's why we're starting in Tokyo – the best possible place to start with a concept for a new game. Who knows, we might get lucky." Frannie kept her head down, busying herself with gathering toiletries now.

"How long will you be gone?"

"I really don't know. Maybe ages."

Frannie raised her tear-filled eyes to Alana and the girls embraced each other, holding the hug for as long as they could to defer their separation.

A knock on the door broke their hug and Simon said "We'd better be off, Babe."

Squeezing Alana's hand, Frannie slung her bag over her shoulder, and left the house with Simon, his arm slung protectively over her shoulder. Alana watched them go with a heavy feeling in the pit of her stomach.

**

The next day Alana gazed at herself in the mirror, assessing her body shape, her face. She was more than aware of the traits that she lacked but she wanted to know whether she could make any changes to enhance any qualities that she may have. She must have some attributes, surely? She and Francesca were non-identical twins, sharing some characteristics but could never be confused for one another.

She was twenty-two years old and had limited experience with boyfriends, a couple of exploratory kisses in high school, and a couple of short-lived romances during university. Listening to her friends totting up their number of sexual conquests humiliated her, and she was envious of the reactions Frannie created in the male company whenever she entered a room. What was it that she lacked? She loved her friends dearly, but she was also realistic – they were not beautiful, and their bodies were not perfect. But still, they had been on the receiving end of numerous flirtations, been on many dates, and had racked up more experience within the last year than she had in her whole life thus far.

Stripped down to her underwear, she turned to look at her profile. Her legs were short, a little heavy in the thighs; her lower abdomen was soft and slightly rounded. Her posture was good – she never slouched or held her pelvis forward, - with heels her legs could be made to look longer and her stomach less pronounced. Her upper arms were not smooth-skinned like Frannie's but rough to the touch and slightly blotchy. She was self-conscious of this and tried to avoid baring her arms.

Her hair was curly, unruly, and mousy blonde, whereas Frannie's was golden blonde with barely a kink. Alana's curls were not spiralled and long, but rather mid-length and slightly bushy. She was not skillful in controlling her hair, too quickly surrendering and resigning herself that 'it will do.' Perhaps this was a change she could make.

Turning to face the mirror, she stepped forward and peered at her face, her eyes immediately drawn to the broken veins in her cheeks. Her eyes were a fairly nondescript colour, somewhere between blue and grey. Her eyebrows were sparse and her lips were full. She wore glasses with a heavy frame, which suited her face.

One thing people had always commented on was her smile, which was wide and genuine. But clearly not attractive enough to the opposite sex! She needed to do something because she could feel her self-confidence taking a nose-dive, and it was never high to begin with! Frannie's unexpected and fearless decision to fly off to Japan at a moment's notice had only served to underline how mousey and safe Alana had always been.

It was time she made some changes!

Getting dressed and slinging a notebook into her bag, Alana set off to get some sun in the quad. Finding a nice spot on the soft grass, removing her shoes, and taking out her notebook and pen, she rolled onto her tummy. Supporting her chin with her hand she watched a group of students larking around, a bunch of first years approaching the end of the academic year with relief. To her right, a group of three female students discussed their plans for the holidays. The campus is quieter now that the third years have completed their courses, Frannie being one of them. Alana's English literature and Spanish course still had a further year to go.

Alana began to write a list:

1. Learn to master my hair. Take a course? Commit to more regular hair appointments?
2. Begin to wear make-up more often to hide the broken veins.
3. With all of the above – build more confidence. Men are attracted to confident women.

Distracted by the sound of muttering and swearing under the breath, Alana raised her head and saw a vaguely familiar man emptying his briefcase onto the picnic table, panic rising.

"Where the hell can it be? It must be here somewhere!"

Pushing herself into sitting Alana watched the man with a frown, her vague memory beginning to sharpen - this was one of Frannie's professors. She remembered Frannie pointing him out to her and laughing, saying that she was aware that his gaze would fall on her slightly more often, and for longer, than the rest of the class. It was fairly well-acknowledged and the students found it amusing and slightly creepy in equal measure. Frannie didn't care – she was used to this sort of attention and she enjoyed the power it gave her.

As Alana watched the professor push his hair back from his face, she remembered that there had been some excitement around the campus about something he had been working on. A new game, that was it. He'd shared the concept with some of the students, had been testing it on a small group and was preparing a pitch with a major company that had already produced the most well-known video games out there. It would be a huge global nod to the university and would make the professor a very rich man.

Rising to her feet, Alana approached the professor.

"Are you ok, sir? Can I help you?"

The professor was now sitting slumped on the picnic bench, the contents of his bag emptied onto the table. He didn't answer but stared ahead as if he did not see her.

"Sir? Professor?"

"She took it. It's all gone."

Alana's phone pinged and she brought it out of her pocket. It was a picture on Instagram from Frannie, her arm around the professor's shoulder, her lips puckered as she kissed him on his cheek. Si could be seen in the background, watching, always watching. Alana felt dizzy - she now knew what her sister had done. Below the picture, Frannie had written "Sorry". She felt the colour drain from her face and could feel the beat of her heart hammering against her rib cage.

"Professor?" she whispered.

"I've been such a damn fool. Idiot!" he berated himself and Alana slipped away, leaving him to his private devastation.

Frannie would not be back. Alana would have nobody to shelter behind anymore, it was time for her to emerge from the shadows, to be her own person, no longer the 'ying' to another's 'yang'. Walking slowly to her belongings on the grass, she picked up her notebook, thought for a moment, turned a page, and wrote at the top

"Who am I, really?"

Love divided by two

Joe was the last person on earth I expected to do that. Joe, my oldest friend was the person I had always trusted most in the world. We had an agreement. It wasn't even an unspoken agreement – it was something that we'd talked about, something we'd vowed never to do to one another. Ex-girlfriends were strictly off-limits. No stepping over that boundary, or it would just get too complicated.

Cathy looks stunning. She is sitting further down at the table next to Joe, tilting her head slightly to listen to what he is whispering in her ear. Her beautiful chestnut hair is swept up off her face but a few curls have worked their way loose during the course of the day and now frame her perfectly shaped ear. My hand aches to touch them, to hold her soft, slender neck in my palm, and to bring down my mouth to plant tender kisses onto the base of her neck and inhale her scent. She's looking down, shyly smiling, and she is oblivious to me. And so is Joe.

I stand up roughly, almost overturning the flimsy table that is balanced on the grass. I head over to the bar for another drink to take my mind off the past and the betrayal playing out before me. While the barman is preparing my drink, I feel a friendly slap on my shoulder…

"Hey mate. I need a drink! All this cheesy smiling is making my cheeks ache."

I turn to look at Joe - tall, gangly even, with blonde hair. In profile, his nose is as straight as a Roman road, the line continuing uninterrupted from his brow to the tip. At school, the girls used to say he was like a Roman god. Joe would laugh it off but he liked the attention, of course he did. Who wouldn't? Being friends with Joe hadn't done me any harm either, though I had my fair share of admirers too. We'd compared notes, as teenage lads do, but we made a pact. If one of us had been out with a girl, she was ruled out for the other.

I met Cathy at university – I was studying law and she was reading Geography. We were thrown together by being placed in the same digs on campus and became friends pretty quickly. She was funny and would sit on the kitchen table in her pyjamas doing impressions of her lecturers or fellow students. We'd go out drinking or dancing with our other flatmates but always made sure that we were close by each other, looking out for one another. Cathy was tall, about the same height as me when she was wearing heels, but mostly she would be in her bare feet, whether in the flat or dancing in the clubs. She is a free spirit, with a smile that would light up the room.

In those days she was mine. One night she came home from a date with a guy from another flat and knocked on my door. Her make-up had run and it was obvious that she had been crying. She climbed onto my bed and sat cross-legged as she told me that he'd come on a bit strong to her, and tried to force her beyond where she wanted to go. She'd managed to escape unharmed but was pretty shaken up. I was suddenly consumed by the need to protect her. The intensity of my feelings for her surprised me. I was torn between storming out of the flat and punching the guy in the face, or taking her in my arms. I sat on the bed next to her and pulled her close into a hug as she sobbed. She didn't go to her room that night – we lay, fully clothed, on the bed and I held her in my arms all night.

In the morning, I was watching her when she opened her eyes. She smiled and leaned forward, kissing me on the lips. I pulled her in close and the kiss went on and on. The taste of her lips against mine was intoxicating. Her smell unleashed some animal instinct and I rolled her onto her back. She did not resist but held me close. As we undressed I felt her urgency matching mine and we became one in a glorious union, and it felt as it had never felt before. At that moment I realised that I was in love with her. The morning extended into a full weekend where we barely left the bed and revelled in discovering each other's bodies and innermost thoughts. I never wanted it to end, but of course, it did, and Cathy returned to her studies. Over the next couple of weeks, she began to withdraw a little, before eventually knocking on my door one evening and asking if she could come in. She seated herself at the chair at my desk and carefully proceeded to destroy me, one organ at a time.

"We're such good friends, you and I – I can get a boyfriend anytime, but friends like you are so hard to find. I don't want to lose you," she said, piercing my skin with the precision of a surgeon's scalpel.

"It's been so great, and I do love you, but as a friend, you see." She went on, her beautiful hand reaching into my chest and taking my heart in its grip.

"So, can we just go back to how we were? It'll be better for both of us, don't you see?" She sat on my study chair with my heart in her hand, blood dripping to the floor as the beats died against her palm.

"If that's what you want, of course," I said, hating myself and hating her at that moment.

She jumped to her feet, put her arms around me, gave me a sisterly hug and kiss on the cheek, then bounced out of the room, obviously feeling lighter having had 'the awkward conversation'. I remained seated, numb. I had tasted love, but now the taste was bitter. I developed an immunity then that led to many meaningless conquests. On the occasional get-together with Joe, I would keep things light. To be fair, I've never told him of my feelings about

Cathy. Never told him of our time together – to him she was an old flatmate of mine, so I guess he didn't feel that he had broken our teenage pact, but that didn't stop me from hating him.

"Yeah, well, you signed up for it. No going back now." I replied to Joe, shaking myself into the present and accepting my drink from the barman.

"Speeches soon," he shouted after me. "Hope you're ready with that Best Man speech!"

Returning to my seat beside Cathy's mum, I felt in my pocket for the sheets of paper with my speech. Immediately she began talking to me, telling me about the first time Cathy had introduced Joe to her family.

"He was so nervous," she giggled, "I don't know what he must have been expecting from us. What Cathy must have told him, I don't know!"

Her voice is sleep-inducing, as monotonous and unending as the sound of a train running along tracks, never changing in rhythm or tone. As she continues with her unbroken monologue, I find myself drifting, only semi-conscious, her words devoid of meaning or function.

Cathy has stood and is leaning over one of her bridesmaids. I can see the sheen of her skin glistening in the sunlight next to the intricate lace pattern of her dress. Her shoulders are bare and I can remember kissing them, lifting her hair to one side to allow access. The dress is corseted and her hourglass figure is imprisoned within. My fingers ache to release the satin ties along the length of her back to free her body from its confinement, mirroring my urge to find some way to liberate her from this marriage that she has entered which can only bring hurt and disappointment.

She takes her seat as the speeches are announced. Joe rises

to his feet, a broad grin across his face, the cat that got the cream. I want to punch him. A strong breeze causes a Mexican wave amongst the trees encircling the area and I feel betrayed even by them, who prefer him to me, just as Cathy does. As the trees wave, I listen to the whispering leaves, rustling urgently, as if telling their secrets. Well, I have some secrets too. Perhaps now is the time to share them, let Cathy know what she is getting into here.

Joe has never been one to think about consequences. From being boys, it's always been me that has to pick up the pieces Joe has left behind him. The time Joe had asked a plain girl at school to the Prom as a bet with the other lads, but then didn't go through with it. He'd ended up with the prettiest girl in the year and it was me that felt sorry for the plain girl and took her along. I can't even remember her name now. Then there was the time Joe had taken up a better offer and stood a girl up, making some excuse that he had taken me to the hospital. I went along with all the lies because he was my mate, and that's what you do. More recently, he found himself in a bit of a fix with a girl he'd got pregnant. She was refusing to get a termination and I was roped in to use my persuasive skills and convince her that she didn't want to get caught up with any long-term commitments to him. But then he had met Cathy, quite accidentally, and they were already quite serious before I even found out. It was too late and too awkward to tell him about my feelings for her and our history. I had hoped it would fizzle out and Joe would move on like he always has. But it hadn't, he didn't and here we are. Well, maybe now it was time for the truth.

"And finally, I want to mention my best mate here," Joe motioned towards me, smiling. "I can tell you, we go back a long way. We've been through a lot together, and I'll be honest, he's got me out of a lot of scrapes, many of them I am not proud of."

Joe held my gaze. I was expecting a wink, a hint of laddishness, but instead, he was dead serious.

"Not only is he my Best Man, he is the very Best of Mates, not only to me but to Cathy too. We are so lucky to have you, mate. We go back a long way, and I love you."

A cheer and a few whistles; everybody applauding and looking at me.

"I hope you will always be part of our lives. I've cleaned my act up a lot since I met Cathy, but I still need you there by my side. Raise a glass to the Best Man in the room!!"

Joe and Cathy raised their glasses. They were so happy. I loved them both and hated them both for making me love them. I stood, raised my glass, and took out the papers from my pocket.

"Thank you. Thank you, Joe. Now let me tell you something you probably don't know about my mate Joe….."

Is it just me?

Extracts from a journal

January

Today I flirted with a man half my age in the Pharmacy while collecting my prescription. Well, I say, flirted - it was unintentional. Recently, I have suspected that my script for my glasses is no longer correct. Either that or my diabetes is playing up. Whatever the reason, it's not significant for my inadvertently trying to proposition an unsuspecting young man! As in most Pharmacies, there are numerous shelves behind the counter displaying those medications which have to be requested, and in between each shelf is a little strip of mirror, presumably so the shop assistant can enjoy watching the frustration of the customer as she or he slowly glides their fingers along the colourful boxes in search of the item which the customer can see directly in front of them! In my case though, the assistant was on her knees below the counter, searching for the prescription, when she had only texted me half an hour ago to say it was ready! To pass the time I thought it would be a good opportunity to test my vision by trying to read the boxes on the shelves, first with only my right eye, and then with my left. Not being able to quite decide how well each eye was performing I continued in this fashion for several minutes then noticed there was a slightly startled young man standing beside me, shuffling his feet and trying to avoid looking at my reflection winking back at him. The assistant emerged triumphantly from beneath the counter, my prescription in her hand, I turned on my heel, smiled at the embarrassed young man, and swept through the door!

It wasn't many days later that I committed another pharmaceutical-based faux pas, this time with a friend. Sitting in a pub we were discussing our various health challenges over a glass of gin. Perhaps this made me a little giddy and reckless because as my friend was sharing her horror at her doctor suggesting that she should begin taking Viagra to help with her circulation, I quipped "But you don't have the appendage that would make it embarrassing, all that would happen to you is that you might keep suddenly raising your arm above your head!" My other friend found this highly amusing and we giggled like a couple of naughty school girls, me feeling rather proud of my witticism, but the person for whom this was a very real concern did not share our mirth. Note to self - beware of a tongue loosened by an unaccustomed glass of gin.

April

"Does your husband worry about you going out on your own?" asked my friend recently. This was said in jest but had been prompted by my regaling her with a tale about my journey home from the city centre by tram. Embarking on the journey, I had prepared myself for a commute of thirty-five minutes - long enough to enjoy my book, so I settled into a quiet, forward-facing seat, texted my husband that I was on my way, and withdrew my book from my bag. Occasional glances at the display screen as the journey progressed kept me oriented and then I noted that the screen read 'Radcliffe', one station from my destination, which was the terminus. "Great," I thought, "I'll just finish this chapter."

A short while later my husband rang my mobile.

"Where are you? I thought you were on the tram that just

came in?"

Glancing at the display I said confidently, "I'm at Radcliffe."

"Oh, right, I'll just wait for the next one then," he said, sounding a little confused.

I turned my attention back to my book, but a moment later had the strangest realisation – somehow, I was no longer forward-facing! How did that happen? The display still read 'Radcliffe'. I was confused. Turning to a gentleman across the aisle on my right, I said,

"Excuse me, did the tram arrive in Bury?"

"Yes," he smiled, indulgently. "Did you miss it? We're on our way back to the city centre now."

I jumped to my feet and alighted when the tram stopped and rang my husband.

"Where are you?" he said.

"Radcliffe"

"Why do you keep saying Radcliffe?" he said, somewhat exasperated.

"I'll explain when I get home. I'll be there in ten minutes, and I won't be getting my book out!"

July

I can't be the only person who has found herself having to follow through with a minor deception in order to save face. Ok, I'll admit it - tell an untruth. There, I've said it, but I'm sure you would agree there really was no other option in the circumstances.

It was a very sunny, hot day and I needed to withdraw some money from the ATM. I was struggling to read the options because of the blinding glare on the glass and had consequently already spent more than my acceptably allocated time at the machine - the queue was growing restless. Glancing over my shoulder, I smiled apologetically to the man behind me as I tucked the crisp banknotes into my purse. But where was my bank card? In a panic, I shielded my eyes to attempt to read the screen which was impossible with the strong sunlight.

"It's taken my card!" I explained to the queue.

I leaned closer to the screen, hand above my head trying to create a shadow over it.

"I'm sorry, it's just not here."

"Did it give you your money?" asked a helpful lady, two people behind the scowling man at the front of the queue.

"Yes, I have the money."

"Well, it must have given you the card back then, because it does that before you get the money."

I slipped my fingers into my handbag, and there it was, nestled in its usual place in the zipped compartment at the back. But how could I own up so publicly to such stupidity?

"No," I said, "it isn't here."

My mind was working ten to a dozen to think how I could

save face when I saw someone in uniform approaching me. Not a police uniform but that of the very helpful staff in the bank.

"Can I help you?" she asked.

"The machine seems to have taken my card," I blurted out.

"Did it give you the money you asked for?"

"Yes", I replied with a sigh, turning my back towards the onlookers. I knew what was coming next.

"So it must have given you the card first then, Madam. Have you checked your handbag?"

I feigned looking in my handbag, taking my time for better effect, before exhaling a quiet breath and answering "Oh yes, it's here. I must have put it there without realising. Thank you so much."

I didn't dare turn to face the queue of people, which had grown considerably, and darted away in the opposite direction to that which I had planned in my haste to escape.

September

My husband is a patient man. Some would say he's had to learn that after being married to me for 36 years. I cannot deny it! He is a man of many, many talents, but like all of us, he has his limitations. Let me tell you about our bedroom ceiling fan as an example. Like many ladies my age, nightly challenges with my own microclimate can become exhausting and I had the bright idea of installing a ceiling fan above the bed in the spare room to provide refuge during particularly difficult nights.

This was definitely a two-man job!

The first mistake was beginning the installation at 8 pm. What the neighbours living in the sheltered accommodation flats opposite must have made of us is anyone's guess, but I think we must have provided some entertainment.

After completing the wiring side of it, my husband required me to take the weight of the thing while he connected it to the ceiling. It must have been as heavy as a small elephant and I had to stand on the bed whilst holding it aloft. Now our bed is not a water bed, but when standing toward the corner of the mattress, it did not know how to adjust to this unanticipated expectation of its springs and proceed to move around beneath me, meaning I felt like a circus clown balancing on a ball. I probably exceeded my nightly sweat count by four times in the installation of this gadget that I hoped would be my saviour!

Finally, my husband went downstairs to the fuse board, needing to use his phone torch as by now it had grown dark around us.

"Ok, switch the light on now!" he called.

I pulled the cord; the light flickered twice then went off.

"Hm," my husband said, " I think I know what's wrong."

After a quick costume change for me into my nightie, we endured a further half hour of my balancing on a rolling ball, holding the fan aloft while he attached said fan, wearing his head torch. By now, the neighbours were probably finishing their popcorn as they watched the show and passed comments on my knee-length nightie which was now mid-thigh as I held my arms above me, doing what must have looked like a belly dance in the beam of my husband's headtorch!

Finally, my husband disappeared down the stairs to the fuse box and, da-dah, the light, and the fan worked. WooHoo.

We celebrated with a cup of tea downstairs.

Half an hour later we decided to go to bed - my fan feels wonderful as I lie here beneath the cool breeze, but I do feel for my husband - he has already stubbed his toe twice in the darkness of our marital bedroom, which, like the rest of the rear of the house, is now without electricity!

Printed in Great Britain
by Amazon

31634675R00076